gaffer tape, pliers and a wayward dog

This book is dedicated to
Jo Forbes – my sister-in-law –
but most importantly a dear
friend, who has been such a
warrior in her fight
against cancer.

gaffer tape, pliers and a wayward dog

by vivian head

Introduction

The rain beat against the windowpane in the tiny grey miner's cottage in Aclare, County Sligo; a constant reminder that it was situated on the Wild Atlantic Way. The place itself was steeped in history even down to a roundabout in the main town that was constructed around a megalithic tomb. For this reason it was very popular with tourists but not today, no one would be brave enough to venture out on the spectacular rugged landscape today. The wind was so strong it was difficult to stay on your feet and the rain fell persistently which was why Findlaech was finding it hard to get out of bed.

He wasn't the sort of person who leapt out of bed each morning in gay abandon, it took at least two cups of strong tea before he had the enthusiasm to face the day. Today, a Monday morning at the beginning of September, he was on his third cup and still couldn't face pulling back the curtains.

Findlaech Doyle was a loner, a solitary figure, who no one really got to know. The locals called him *aestech*, which translated into 'strange, bizarre' but that didn't bother him. He didn't care what other people thought of him as long as they left him alone. Up until a year ago he had shared the tiny cottage with his younger brother, Byrne, but Ankou, the god of death, had taken him in his prime. Findlaech had become withdrawn, barely leaving the *feirme bheag*, or smallholding, totally overcome by grief. He allowed his mourning to take over his entire existence and yet not a tear was shed.

1 Dark Days

Byrne was a popular young man, rugged in appearance, with a handsome head of coarse, straw-coloured hair. His pale blue eyes attracted the attention of the local lasses, but Byrne had always been loyal to his brother who had raised him since he was seven years old. He had always felt guilty if he spent the evening down the local tavern, only too aware that his brother was at home alone. His friends had told him that he had to start living his own life; he needed to break free. He told them one day he would have the strength to leave but not yet, not while his brother needed him. He lost count of how many times they told him to go. He also lost count of how many times he was told his brother was no good for him. But Byrne was devoted and tried to comprehend the constant melancholy that followed Findlaech around.

Findlaech thought back to the night his mother passed away. He had never known his father, and Birte, which meant powerful and strong, lived up to her name. She had raised her two boys, looked after the feirme and always made sure there was food on the table.

Both boys had attended Castlerock Primary School that boasted just fifty-nine pupils. They were raised in the Catholic faith and taught to be respectful, kind and gentle people. Byrne thrived in the small local community, but Birte despaired of her eldest son who barely spoke a word and was unable to make eye contact with anyone including herself. She sought help from the family physician, Doctor Donoghue, but he just said the lad was shy and that one day he would find his feet. 'You are worrying over nothing, Birte, you wait and see.' There were indeed some good days, but the bad days were really bad.

Findlaech was never happier than when he was tending their small flock of goats and sheep. His greatest joy was to help with the milking and assist his mother in making the beautiful fresh cheese she was renowned for. His strongest bond, apart from his mother, was with their sheepdog Boxty, named after his mother's delicious pancakes. Every day after he had done his chores the pair would race off to the ruins of Belclare Castle where Boxty would chase birds and Findlaech would pretend to be King of Sligo.

Life, however, dealt Findlaech a bitter blow on the night of 4 August following a phone call at around nine-thirty. He watched as his mother's brow furrowed in concern, gripping the handset tightly until her knuckles whitened. Two of their beloved sheep had become trapped on a ledge on the edge of the mountain that stood behind their land. Birte had gone out armed with a flashlight and rope, accompanied by their closest neighbours, instructing the boys to stay put until she returned.

'You'll not be answering the door to anyone, do you hear me,' she said before leaving and braving the strong winds. Boxty accompanied her on her mission, but three hours later they had not returned and the boys were starting to fret. They sat huddled together in the front room, listening to the wind whipping around the old stone cottage.

They both jumped when they heard a knock at the door. They were under strict instructions to open the door to no one, but the knocks were persistent and someone was shouting their names.

Byrne, the braver of the two, eventually went up to the front door.

'And who might be out there,' he said in his broad Irish lilt.

''Tis Mr Ceallaigh from Glen Beag Farm. Now will you be opening the door boys?'

Byrne knew Mr Ceallaigh well because he always dropped his daughter off at the school gates in his tractor, so he felt it was safe to open the door.

Standing behind Mr Ceallaigh was his rather portly wife, Meabh, who immediately walked through the doorway and went into the kitchen.

'Will you be having a cup of tea?' she asked no one in particular.

'Aw, go on then, there's nothing that can't be solved with a cup of tea,' Mr Ceallaigh said, indicating for the two brothers to sit down.

'Now 'tis bad news I'm having to bring you, boys,' he said, taking off his flat cap and wiping it across his forehead. 'Your ma has taken a tumble off Keshcorran trying to rescue your sheep.'

'Is it bad?' Byrne asked.

''Tis real bad, lad,' he said.

Findlaech had said nothing and just continued to look down at his hands. He was fiddling with a piece of fringe on the old woollen blanket used to cover a hole in the sofa. 'Where's Boxty?' he eventually said.

'Aw, lad, Boxty went over too. He was doing what any good

sheepdog should do, he was trying to rescue his flock.'

Byrne collapsed into floods of tears, causing Meabh to come out of the kitchen and take him in her arms. He buried his head in her buxom bosom and cried until he eventually fell asleep.

Findlaech remained silent. No tears, no words, just lost in his own very dark thoughts.

'You can come and live with us,' Meabh said without a second thought.

'We'll be fine thank you, Mrs Ceallaigh,' Findlaech said finally finding his voice. 'I'm fifteen now. I will be the man of the house and take care of my brother.'

Meabh looked at her husband, tears welling up in her eyes. 'Well, if that is what you want, lad, then I'll no be stopping you.'

Findlaech nodded and assured them they would be fine.

'I know all about running the feirme, me ma taught me, and I can sell the milk and cheese for money to pay the bills.' All his conversation was directed at the floor; not once did he look up.

'Well, lad, if you are sure. But you have to let us help. Meabh here will bring you down some pies and I will take Byrne to school until you get on your feet.'

Findlaech nodded again.

'Thank you,' he said, remembering he had always been taught to be polite.

2 The Dark Mist

Life drifted by and eventually the pain of their mother's loss waned enough for them to move on with their lives. Byrne grew into a strong, positive young man who looked up to his older brother. Findlaech, however, became more and more withdrawn only leaving the feirme to visit the market; more out of necessity than any desire to meet people.

The neighbours stopped paying visits, although Byrne did remain good friends with the Cellaigh's daughter, Niamh. Everyone believed Findlaech was beyond help and gradually gave up on him. It seemed only natural to turn away from someone who showed no interest in helping himself.

Findlaech never stopped his younger brother from seeing his friends, never even made any comment. Sometimes Byrne took it as indifference and that perhaps he was just a burden. This was far from the truth, in reality Findlaech wanted his brother to live his life to the fullest; after all he hadn't been inflicted with the dreadful depressions that darkened his life. One day he would wake up full of optimism, get out of bed early, make breakfast and then get all his chores done before midday. But the next day the dark mist descended and he could barely drag one foot in front of another. Those were the days when he didn't want his brother to see him, so he always encouraged him to go out and enjoy himself.

Byrne knew his brother wasn't like him. He was like two

different people. He had heard of people suffering from 'the dreaded depressions' but he had no idea how to help him. He tried talking to him, tried helping him on the feirme, but each time Findlaech would tell him he could manage and that he should go off out and see his friends. And so that is what Byrne used to do. He tried to block out his brother's dark moods but he never stopped caring.

One night Byrne had one too many glasses of stout down the local pub. Although it wasn't strictly a pub in the sense of the word, but one of the locals had managed to get a licence to sell alcohol and converted his front room into a snug. As soon as the night air hit him, Byrne found it hard to walk in a straight line and his head was spinning like a top. He stumbled several times, but somehow always managed to get himself up and continue his journey home on his rickety old bike. The final fall happened on the stony path that led down the cliff towards the feirme. The front wheel hit a large rock and he fell over the handlebars, hitting his head on an old piece of metal that was concealed under a tuft of coarse grass. The metal penetrated his skin causing a deep gouge in his forehead. The alcohol numbed the pain, but by the time he reached the cottage the blood was pouring down his face and had stained the front of his sweater.

'Now what have you gone and done?' Findlaech said as Byrne stumbled in through the door.

Byrne was past being able to answer and collapsed on the floor.

Findlaech lifted his brother off the floor, laid him on his bed, removed his clothes and then bathed him lovingly like a baby, removing every trace of blood. He bandaged the wound on his head and decided he would call the doctor in the morning. He spent the night with his brother just to make sure he was all right, something he hadn't done since they stopped sharing a room.

The next day Byrne was finding it hard to lift his head off the pillow. His arms and legs felt like lead and his head was thumping. Findlaech put it down to the amount of ale he had drunk the night before, but decided he would call Doctor Donoghue just to be on the safe side. His brother was young, healthy and would soon be back on his feet. He couldn't have been more wrong. By that evening his temperature was so high he was delirious. By the time the doctor arrived, around eight-fifteen, Byrne was barely conscious.

'What happened to him, Findlaech?'

'He came home drunk last night but managed to tell me he had fallen on the lane.'

'Do you know what caused the cut on his head?' he asked.

'No, not really, you see it was dark when he came off his bike.'

'Well, you did a good job of bathing it, but I fear he has got an infection which has gone into his blood.'

'Is that bad, doc?' he asked fearfully.

'Aye, lad, it can be real bad.'

By two-thirty that morning Byrne had lost the fight, despite the concoction of antibiotics administered by the doctor his body had given into the sepsis.

The dark depressions Findlaech was already experiencing became worse, until the good days were few and far between. And today, being a wet Monday, was as bad as they came.

3 Findlaech's Ark

Riley Ceallaigh had been concerned about the O'Connor boys ever since their mother had died, but he couldn't deny Findlaech did everything he could for his younger brother. Now that Byrne had gone, the Ceallaigh's knew they could no longer stay away; the young man needed their help. Findlaech had always been strange and now, in his late twenties, he had become a total recluse. Several times his wife, Meabh, had tried to go down to the feirme and offer him some of her succulent pies but he either didn't answer the door or, if he was working outside, he would just ask her to leave it on the kitchen table. That was the only time they got to see him.

When Niamh got married they invited Findlaech to the wedding in the hope he would come out of his shell. Riley even went to the cottage to lend him a suit, but Findlaech was a closed book, only opening the door a crack, declining their kind offer.

He was always polite, it wasn't that he was rude; it was just that he didn't want to see people. People made him uncomfortable. He couldn't think of anything worse than going to a wedding, even if it was one of his relatively good days, because it would mean he would have to make conversation and conversation was the one thing he was really bad at.

He found he could always talk to the animals. Animals were not a problem and he felt a close affinity with them all. Animals did not ask awkward questions, animals did not make him feel uncomfortable, no, quite the opposite. He would talk to his sheep, talk to his goats, talk to his two chickens and even talk to the little robin that used to sit on the fence post while he was tilling the soil.

Despite the inclement weather, Findlaech managed to grow a good crop of vegetables and once a fortnight he would take the old handcart, load it up with potatoes, onions, carrots, turnips, beets and whatever else was in season and take them down to the local market along with any spare milk and cheese. He didn't have the confidence to sell his produce, but one of Byrne's friends had a market stall and was only too happy to sell it for him. He found he had all the money he needed for his meagre existence.

Friday was market day, which meant he had a week to tend to his feirme. Milk and cheese were his main source of income and cheese didn't make itself. He had loads of jobs to do but today he couldn't face getting up. When the 'depressions' hit him hard, the world was a very dark place. Many a time he had thought about taking his own life, but he was a coward and scared that it wouldn't work and he would be left in an even worse state.

If only it wasn't raining today, he thought. It was just another excuse not to get out of bed. Then he heard the sound of one of the goats bleating and it tugged at his heartstrings, thinking of them out in the rain. He had built them a shelter, but on days like today, they needed more than just a makeshift shack to keep them dry and warm.

Findlaech had always been good with his hands. When he had been at school his teacher had told his mother he excelled in woodwork and that he should pursue it as a career. Had circumstances turned out differently, Findlaech would have loved to work in wood, but his only concern now was to keep the homestead going in memory to his mother and brother who had been his entire world.

He had been too lazy to take off all his clothes the night before, so he had spent the night in his old work clothes and when he pulled off the eiderdown his mother had lovingly made, he felt disgusted with himself. How could he let himself get like this? How had he ever sunk so low when the animals depended on him? He may not have a brother anymore, but the animals were like his children and they were the only things that gave him the will to live.

Doctor Donoghue had given him some pills to take on his very worst days, but they made him feel sleepy and sluggish so he tried not to take them. They did not lift his dark moods, the dark fog that filled his brain; they just made it grey instead of black.

Eventually dragging himself downstairs, Findlaech grabbed his sou'wester off the back of the door and his wellies from the flagstones that covered the floor in the tiny porch. He opened the door to the cottage, bent down to avoid hitting his head on the lintel, and braced himself against the relentless wind and rain. He crossed the yard to the shelter cobbled together with bits of wood and corrugated iron. All the animals were delighted to see him and started to nuzzle at his legs with their noses, trying to encourage him to give them some food.

'Not yet, my lovelies, let's get you dry first,' he said, giving one of the sheep a rub on the top of his head.

Last week had been beautiful sunny weather and he had taken advantage and sheared his eight sheep. He gathered the wool into large sacks, put it into his handcart and took it to Glen Beag Farm. Meabh Ceallaigh had a spinning wheel and turned the wool into the most beautiful balls of yarn. She either made them into sweaters, rugs, blankets, hats, gloves, scarves or simply sold the yarn to other women in Sligo.

Meabh was quite shocked to see Findlaech. He very rarely left the feirme and she gave him a beaming smile as he walked up her front path. She was working on her spinning wheel in the sunshine at the front of their cottage (or *teachin* as they were more familiarly known).

'Why Findlaech, it's lovely to see you,' she said, genuinely relieved to see that he was doing okay.

'And you Mrs Ceallaigh. I have some wool for you.'

He removed the sacks of wool from the back of the cart and left them propped up against the wall.

'I'll tell you how much it's worth once I have it weighed,' she told him.

'Thank you Mrs Ceallaigh.'

That was the extent of their conversation before he felt the need to leave and return to the safety of his own land. It took all the willpower he could summon up to actually leave the feirme and interact with people even if he knew them well.

'Ah, Findlaech, wouldn't you be liking a cup of tea?' she asked hopefully as he turned his back.

'No, I'll be on my way, Mrs Ceallaigh,' he said without turning around, simply waving his hand in the air.

She sighed a deep sigh. He was such a polite young man,

a good-looking young man in a rough kind of way, he would make someone a wonderful husband, she thought. But then she remembered Byrne talking about his 'depressions' and she wondered if any woman would be able to put up with him and his funny ways. Still, that didn't mean she would stop trying.

Because the sheep had been sheared the rain had penetrated their skin and some of them were shivering in the chill autumn wind. He ushered them across the yard along with the goats and four ducks into his extremely small kitchen. The old Aga was burning and the room was lovely and warm. The animals were a little confused for a while, but once Findlaech had put down some bowls of food and water and made up areas where they could sleep, they started to settle. His kind, gentle voice had a soothing effect on them and instead of panicking and rushing around like mad things, they made themselves comfortable, glad to be out of the storm.

'Now that's better, isn't it, my beauties,' he said looking around proudly.

It didn't matter to him that the floor was now soaking wet, a mixture of rain, animal faeces and feed. These creatures were all that mattered to him because if he didn't have them to depend on him for survival he would be totally lost. He looked around him and realised the depression had lifted slightly and he put the old tin kettle on the Aga and waited for it to boil. He made himself an omelette using the onions he had grown, the wild mushrooms he foraged from one of the meadows and eggs that Matilda and Freda dutifully laid for him each morning.

He sat down at the kitchen table that was littered with pieces of paper, tools and onions that were drying before being put into storage. He pushed Freda off with one arm and was about to take a mouthful when someone knocked on the door. He wondered who on earth it could be because nobody bothered to come to his feirme any more.

From where he was sitting he was clearly visible from the small window situated next to the front door. He got up quickly before anyone looked in and flattened himself against the natural stone wall. Breathing deeply he prayed the animals would remain quiet.

The knocking became more persistent and he recognised Mrs Ceallaigh's voice calling his name.

He stayed perfectly still hardly daring to breath. Please, please go away, he thought, he really couldn't face anyone today.

But Mrs Ceallaigh was not easily put off and instead of waiting for Findlaech she pushed the door open and called his name again.

Findlaech knew it was useless to ignore her any longer and he really didn't want her coming into the kitchen so he stepped into the porch pretending he hadn't heard her.

'Findlaech, sorry to bother you,' Meabh said with a big smile on her ruddy face, 'only I bought your money round for that wool you brought me, I thought you might need it.'

'That's very kind Mrs Ceallaigh,' trying to push the door closed before she could see the state of his kitchen.

She let out a small scream as a goat pushed through the small gap and straight through her legs, knocking her backwards, pushing all the air out of her lungs.

She lay gasping like a fish out of water, her cheeks even redder than before.

'Oh Mrs Ceallaigh, I'm so sorry.'

Findlaech put an arm under each of her armpits and pulled and pulled trying to get her to her feet. He was quite a strong man but Mrs Ceallaigh was such a great weight he struggled on the wet ground, his feet slipping from underneath him. Twice she dropped back down to the ground with a bit of a bump, until eventually he managed to get her up and put his arm around her rather large waist and helped her indoors.

'Oh dear, oh dear, I need to sit down,' she said in a bit of a fluster.

Findlaech hated seeing people hurt or upset, especially as he had been the cause. He couldn't do anything but invite her inside and give her a seat and a nice cup of tea.

He led her carefully to the sofa, which luckily wasn't occupied by anyone other than Ferris, a large ginger tomcat that actually belonged to a neighbouring farm but who seemed to prefer his home. He attracted animals like a magnet and this particular cat was in no hurry to leave.

Meabh sat down heavily, and her excessive weight pushed Ferris into the air. He made the most dreadful sound, hissed and then ran off to lie on the chair positioned beside the Aga.

'Oh dear Lord, Findlaech, this place looks like Noah's Ark.'

As she got her breath back she took in more and more of her surroundings and really didn't like what she saw.

'Oh Findlaech, how can you live like this? It's quite appalling, nothing but a pig sty.'

Findlaech was offended by her words, but had to admit

he really had let the place and himself go. And of course the addition of extra animals hadn't helped. He had always allowed Matilda and Freda to come and go as they please, but adding eight sheep, four goats and three geese to the equation had only increased the chaos further. Suddenly he felt ashamed.

Findlaech dropped his head like a small schoolboy receiving a reprimand. 'I only wanted to offer them shelter from the storm,' he mumbled.

'What's that you say, lad, speak up.'

He repeated what he had said, lifting his head slightly so she could hear.

'You're a good lad, Findlaech, but you really need to start looking after yourself. I know you will put up a fight, but tomorrow I am going to come armed with a mop and bucket and loads of bleach and I am going to blitz this house until you don't recognise it.'

'Oh . . . oh . . . that really won't be necessary Mrs Ceallaigh, I can do it.'

Meabh stood up, lifted his chin gently with her hand and looked him straight in the eyes. 'But you won't will you?'

Findlaech had always been taught to be respectful and he didn't want to answer Meabh back. He knew she was only trying to be neighbourly but he would so much prefer it if she would just go away and leave him alone.

'And I know what you're thinking, lad, you want me to go away and forget what I have seen. Well I won't, I won't, I'm telling you. You need help and help you are going to get whether you like it or not. I want all these animals out of here by the morning.'

She pulled her large oilskin cape around her shoulders,

tying the hood securely in place under her chin. She then turned and left without saying another word, waddling up the path fighting against the wind.

Findlaech was left standing in the middle of the mayhem, speechless. How could he have let her see the place in such a complete and utter mess.

He knew Mrs Ceallaigh was right. What would his mother have said? He knew he had to bite the bullet and allow her to come in and clean the cottage. He sat back down with the full intention of eating his omelette, even though he knew it would be cold by now. He was really hungry and his mouth started salivating at the thought, only one of the goats had beaten him to it and the last piece was hanging from the animal's mouth. Findlaech could swear he saw a smile.

Findlaech leaned back, put his hands on hips and laughed out loud. Everything in the kitchen went quiet; Findlaech had not laughed for years and it felt good.

4 The Pact

The storm blew itself out by five o'clock that evening. The sun showed its face and Findlaech was able to get his kitchen back to himself. The animals were quite happy to go back out and munch on the fresh grass that had sprung up due to the rain.

He propped the back door open and fetched a bucket and mop from the scullery. Both were covered in cobwebs and dust, but once rinsed were sufficient for the job. He cleared the kitchen of furniture by putting it out in the yard, filled the bucket with hot water and plenty of disinfectant which he found under the sink, and swilled the floor, pushing the dirty water out the back door after each bucketful. He hadn't bought any cleaning products for years and any that were in the cupboard were left over from the days when his ma was still alive. That was when he realised how long it had been since he had done any housekeeping.

As he swooshed each bucketful of water over the flagstones Findlaech felt the dark fog lifting until it was just a light mist lingering behind his eyelids. He pushed and pushed with the mop, eradicating his 'depressions' with each sweep. He hadn't felt this invigorated for years and he cleaned and cleaned until the floor was spotless.

Ferris, who had stayed and watched him from the windowsill, shook himself, rubbed his paw over his eye a couple of times and then decided it was time to leave. He knew this wasn't the normal behaviour of his adopted owner and he really didn't like the smell of the disinfectant that made his nostrils sting.

Findlaech watched as he skidded across the wet flagstones, almost losing his footing before making a giant leap for the doormat. Findlaech smiled. 'Mind how you go there, Ferris, we don't want you breaking a leg.'

The old radio in the corner was dusty and covered in grease, but it still worked. He turned the knob and then fiddled with the dial until he got a reasonable reception. It crackled a bit but soon an old folk song reverberated around the kitchen and Findlaech started to whistle *Whiskey in the Jar* while he continued his cleaning. He washed everything before bringing it back in, finishing each piece off with a layer of polish.

Even the old Aga shone, the ancient blue paint taking over from the years of grime, as in the days when his ma was alive.

It was dark by the time he had finished and the sickle moon was high in the sky. A combination of bats and swallows were silhouetted against the darkening sky. He stood in the doorway and looked at the results of all his hard work. It was totally unrecognisable from a few hours ago and it felt so good. There was still the little snug to clean, the downstairs bathroom and of course the two bedrooms upstairs, but Findlaech decided he would tackle those in the morning before Mrs Ceallaigh arrived. He stood in the back door, took his old pipe down from the top of the dresser, stuffed the bowl with some fresh tobacco, found some matches in one of the kitchen drawers amongst some string, puffed on the stem until it was truly alight and then blew smoke rings up towards the moon.

His stomach grumbled and he realised he hadn't eaten

anything since breakfast. There was one bowl of vegetable stew in the larder, one piece of sourdough and plenty of fresh butter so he would make do. He never ate anything fancy but what he did make was wholesome and tasty. That evening everything tasted that little bit better and he swore it was because he had done something positive today.

After he had eaten he scoured the old bathtub clean, filled it with hot water and some old bath salts he had found in the cabinet and lay soaking until the water went cold. When he looked in the mirror, his cheeks were flushed and he was shocked to see his blond hair restored to its normal lustre instead of the dull mousey colour from the weeks of dirt that had accumulated in it.

All his old clothes went into the bucket he used as a laundry basket and he decided in the morning he would wash them along with his bed linen and hang them outside to dry. Today had ended up a positive day and he had achieved so much, maybe things would take a turn for the better.

Findlaech fell asleep that night a happy man.

With the dawning of a new day, came the onset of one of the worst periods of desolation and desperation Findlaech had ever experienced. It was as if someone had drawn a thick curtain across his life; not a pinprick of light penetrated the enveloping screen. Findlaech grabbed at the imaginary fabric, trying to stop the sense of suffocation it evoked. His hands flailed, failing to find anything of substance in front of his eyes and he let out a heart-wrenching scream.

It didn't make sense after last night's euphoria, but then that was how his moods hit him. It never made any sense. It never gave him any warning, no time to prepare. He lay face down on the bed, hitting his head as hard as he could into the old feather pillow hoping to experience physical pain instead of this mental torment. Then the tears started. Findlaech never cried. Findlaech never showed emotion. That was when he knew how bad this day was going to be. He pulled his pillow over his head and sunk into his depression, allowing it to pull him under as if he were submerged in water.

Ferris, sensing the man's struggle, wriggled himself up the bed until he could rub his face against Findlaech's head. Usually this would have got a reaction, but not this time, today he was simply pushed away. The cat immediately picked up on his owner's mood, jumped from the bed onto the windowsill and out through the open window. It leapt down onto the flint tiles of the porch below and then sprang off across the meadow in search of breakfast, passing Mrs Ceallaigh coming down the track in her normal swaying gait. He stopped to rub against her leg and she bent, as much as her rotund body would allow, and stroked his back.

'And how's your master this morning?' she asked. 'Grumpy I expect at the thought of me coming round with me mop and bucket.'

She was indeed armed to the gunnels with cleaning paraphernalia of every imaginable kind. She was pulling it behind her in a small handcart her husband had made to carry shopping back from the market. He had offered to drive her, but Meabh declined, saying she really needed to lose some weight and what better way than to walk.

'Are you sure about this, Meabh?' he had said at breakfast. 'You know Findlaech likes to keep himself to himself.'

'I'm as certain as I am that the sun will rise in the morning and the moon in the evening, that's how sure I am, Mr Ceallaigh. I will help that young man even if it kills me in the process.'

'Aw, ma, don't go saying things like that.'

He plonked a kiss on his wife's cheek and passed another slice of buttered toast across the table, which she proceeded to spread liberally with honey taken from their own hives.

'You know I am only talking metaphorically, Riley. That young man is in trouble.'

'In trouble. Why, are the Garda Síochána after him?'

'Oh, Riley, no not the Garda. He is in trouble from his own disturbed mind. Byrne used to talk to our Niamh and told her his brother used to suffer something terrible.'

'Oh, yes, that. But how on earth do you think you can help, ma?'

In truth Meabh wasn't sure she could help. She wasn't sure young Findlaech would allow her to help, or indeed want her interfering, but she was going to have a darned good try anyway.

'Now, da, I'm off. I've left your lunch in the pantry and I will be home in time to cook your tea.'

On arriving at the cottage, Meabh felt inclined to just walk in but out of politeness she rapped several times on the door. After the sixth attempt she gave up and turned the handle. No one ever locked doors in this part of Aclare, there simply wasn't any need.

A strong smell of disinfectant wafted up into her nostrils as soon as the door opened. Meabh was flabbergasted to say the least. In comparison to the day before the kitchen was spotless and there wasn't an animal in sight.

'Well, well, what a turnaround. Well tickle my pinky!' This was a phrase that Meabh was well known for and often caused a little chuckle, especially with the village kids. The last time she had used it had been at the Women's Institute Bazaar when a little bird had landed on top of one of her chocolate cupcakes. It had left two perfect footprints either side of the cherry perched in the centre and after she shooed it off, she simply pressed the icing back into shape and sold it anyway.

'Findlaech!' she called out, repeating it a couple of times when she received no response. She thought perhaps he was out working on the feirme and decided she would make a start with the cleaning anyway.

She took off her jumper, rolled up her sleeves and went and filled her bucket with some nice hot water and a capful of bleach. She was about to make her way into the snug with her broom when she heard a noise coming from upstairs. She wasn't quite sure what she had heard but felt it was worthy of investigation.

The old, crooked stairs creaked as she ascended, hauling herself up by using the banister. As she reached the landing, the sound was discernible as sobbing and she made her way towards the bedroom. The door was half open and when she peered in she saw Findlaech lying on his stomach, his body heaving from the ferocity of his sobs. She was in two minds to turn around and go back downstairs; no one likes to be disturbed when they are crying. Then she realised he was in such a bad way he wasn't even aware of her presence.

She walked slowly over to the side of the bed, knelt down and put her hand on his back. He didn't even flinch at her touch, he was in such a bad place he was not conscious of anything.

'Findlaech, Findlaech,' she spoke gently.

He didn't react in any way, just continued to cry hitting his head violently into the pillow.

She went round the far side of the bed where there was a small table with a drawer and opened it up. She remembered Byrne saying that Doctor Donoghue had prescribed him some medication some time back. Sure enough, nestled away in the back of the drawer were a small brown pot of pills and a rather battered copy of *Wind in the Willows*.

She took out the pills, made sure they had Findlaech's name on them and then went back downstairs to make him a cup of tea. Tea solved everything Meabh believed.

When she returned to the bedroom, the sobbing had ceased but Findlaech still had his face buried in the feather pillow.

'Findlaech, it's me, Meabh.'

At first he didn't respond, he just lay there in silence. Then he took an extremely deep breath and turned to look at her, his eyes were red and swollen and his face a picture of the torture he was suffering.

'Oh Findlaech, you shouldn't go through this alone.'

Overcome by desperation, Findlaech forgot his usual shyness and aversion to physical contact, turning to give Mrs. Ceallaigh an enormous hug. Meabh was so taken aback she was about to say something, but then thought better of it and just let him have his moment of comfort.

After a couple of minutes, she managed to wriggle one arm free and she stroked the top of his hair.

'Findlaech, I want you to take these pills for me,' she said gently.

He lifted his head and looked at her in desperation. 'Will they make me feel better?' he asked.

'Well, they can't make you feel worse and most probably you will want to sleep, but I think that might be good for you.'

He nodded, far too deep in the depths of his depression to want to fight. He swallowed two of the little blue pills and then lay on his back.

'I'm so sorry,' he said starting to cry again. 'You shouldn't have to see me like this.'

'Oh, Findlaech, if only you had let us help you earlier.'

'I don't think anyone can help, Mrs Ceallaigh, I honestly don't. Some days are so bad all I can think about is ending it all. But I am a coward and I don't know how.'

'Aw, lad, that's nay right, that's nay right at all. I tell you what . . .'

He looked at her expectantly, not really knowing what was coming next.

'. . . if you'll help me, then I'll do everything I can to help you.'

'Help you?' he said in amazement. 'How on earth could I help you?'

'Aw, Findlaech, Doctor Donoghue has told me I have to lose some weight because my health is suffering,' she told him.

'I haven't told Riley what he said 'cos he will get mad, and in all honesty I haven't a clue where to begin.'

Findlaech never once considered that other people had problems, his life only revolved around himself and his animals. It hadn't dawned on him that people got sick; when had he ever taken the time to find out?

'Mrs Ceallaigh, I don't know what to say. I have been a selfish and thoughtless young man, wallowing in my own self-pity. Today you have made me realise that there are other people suffering, not just me, and of course I'll try and help you.'

That day they made a pact. No matter how bad the depressions were or how desperate Meabh was to eat another barm brack, they would look out for each other.

The pills were starting to take effect and Findlaech was finding it hard to keep his eyelids open.

Meabh could see he was struggling but said before she would allow him to go to sleep he had to have some breakfast so she made her way back to the kitchen, made him a plate of scrambled eggs and fried tomatoes with hot buttered toast and a fresh cup of nice strong tea. When it was ready she called upstairs and Findlaech came down with a blanket wrapped around his shoulders.

He couldn't remember a time he had enjoyed a meal so much. The food tasted so much better than when he cooked it and he smiled weakly at Meahb.

'I don't think today is going to be such a black day after all.'

Meahb smiled back, her mouth salivating at the sight of the food on his plate. How on earth was she going to stop her craving for food?

Findlaech saw her eyes drop to his plate.

'Mrs Ceallaigh it is going to be hard for both of us. I know that most days I will struggle, and you will too, but you are right together we can beat this.'

After I have slept I am going to get up and make you a really hearty vegetable broth to take home with you. When you crave food you can have a nice bowlful followed by one of the apples from my orchard to take away the craving for something sweet.

Meabh thought of the chicken and leek pie, with rich butter pastry, a dollop of mashed potatoes and roasted carrots she had planned for tonight's tea. She doubted a bowl of vegetable stew and an apple would satisfy her cravings, but then if Findlaech was prepared to try and beat his depressions then she would try her damned hardest to beat her overeating.

'Off to bed with you now. I've got a lot of cleaning to do.' Right at that moment she felt she would do anything to take her mind off food.

5 A Stark Warning

Findlaech slept soundly until five o'clock that evening. He'd had a few strange dreams regarding animals talking to him, but he put that down to the drugs. He expected to feel lethargic and downhearted as he had that morning, but instead he felt as if an enormous weight had been lifted from the top of his head. He rolled his shoulders and was aware the dull ache from constant tension had gone. He quite literally sprung out of bed and went downstairs.

Mrs Cellaigh had worked her magic. Everything was spotless and all his washing had been done and was hanging out on a makeshift washing line across the yard. Even his bedclothes had been removed and washed. How on earth had she done that without him knowing? After their little chat that morning he had seen his neighbour in a different light. He had never considered that she might not be well. In fact he probably hadn't ever given her a second thought.

He knew only too well what a strain that extra weight would be putting on her heart and he was pretty certain her legs were covered in ulcers because she always had them bandaged up. He was surprised her husband hadn't said anything, but possibly he knew her so well he didn't notice she was struggling.

He remembered his promise to make her a vegetable stew and went to his store cupboard to fetch a variety of ingredients. He knew he was probably too late for her tea but he would make sure she had it tomorrow so she could start her new diet.

Findlaech's lifestyle meant he always ate healthily and once again it had never occurred to him that other people were any different. He didn't have any spare money to waste on luxuries, so what he grew or made he ate. He was no baker, so cakes and biscuits were never a problem. His one luxury was the sourdough bread that he purchased from an old telephone box at the end of his lane. It was an honesty box, where you left your money in an old tin can and took what you wanted. There was a telephone number on a card inside, but he really had no idea who made the delicious bread.

Once the stew was made and simmering away on the top of the Aga he went outside to check on his livestock. As always they were pleased to see him and ran across the meadow to greet him. He patted them all on the head and called each one by name. Tomorrow he decided he would get up early and make a proper shelter before winter set in. He had enough pieces of decent wood in his log store to make a start and if he needed more he knew Mr Cellaigh had plenty he could sell him. He had his day planned and he felt good.

The following morning Findlaech fetched his old bike from the behind the shelter, put some air in the tyres and oiled the brake mechanism. It had no gears but it would be adequate to get him to Mrs Cellaigh's farm with the two pots of stew he had made for her. He made sure the caps were tight on the thermos flasks, strapped them securely to the carrier at the back and then set off for Glen Beag Farm.

Although Findlaech was fit, it was quite a struggle riding the bike up the rough track and it wasn't until he got to the smooth road that he started to make some progress.

When he arrived at the door he knocked and waited for someone to answer. Riley Cellaigh answered the door and he looked pale, tired and withdrawn.

'Ah, Findlaech, me lad, what can I do for you?'

'I promised Mrs Cellaigh some of my vegetable stew. Is she around?'

He held out the two flasks for Mr Cellaigh to take, but instead his eyes welled up and he said, 'Meabh was taken to hospital last night with a suspected heart attack.'

'Oh no, surely not. She was with me yesterday and she seemed fine.'

'It happened last night about eight o'clock. She was very out of breath and then she said her chest and arm were hurting her. I had to call an ambulance.'

'Can I go and see her?'

Riley was taken aback at the young man's show of emotion. He had never bothered to interact with either of them before and he thought how out of character it was.

'Well, come in, Findlaech and let me take that stew from you.'

'Thank you, Mr Cellaigh. I feel awful, I fear it may be my fault that your wife is unwell.'

'Why? What do you mean?'

'Well, you see, I got myself in a bit of a state and your lovely wife promised to come over and help me clean the cottage. I think she probably overdid it because by the time I woke up all the work was done, including all my washing.'

'Now don't be blaming yerself, lad. Meabh will only do what she wants to do and she told me how worried she was about you.'

'I still feel guilty, but I really would like to go and see her,' he said trying to keep his composure.

'Visiting isn't until three o'clock I'm afraid and by then we will know more because they are carrying out tests this morning. If you would like to come back this afternoon we can go together in the truck.'

'Thank you Mr Cellaigh, I would like that very much. I will come back at two-thirty if that's okay.'

'That's more than okay, Findlaech, and please call me Riley.' He shook his hand and said he would see him later.

'Oh, before I leave do you have any wood I can buy? I want to make a proper shelter for my livestock, you see.'

'Come and have a look in the barn and see if there is anything suitable,' Riley said, getting his hat and jacket from the hook on the back of the door.

Together they walked up to the Cellaigh's quite substantial barn, divided up into compartments to house his cattle when the weather got too bad. In one corner, tucked behind the large hay bales were several large pieces of wood, perfect for making a new shelter.

'They would be perfect Mr C..., er Riley,' Findlaech said, correcting himself. 'How much would you be wanting for them?'

'I'll be wanting nothing, thank you. It will be nice to know they are being put to good use. If you help me load them on the back of the truck, I'll bring them down to your feirme for you.'

'I don't know how to thank you, Riley,' he said, slightly embarrassed at this show of bonhomie, seeing as he had never made the effort to get to know either of them properly.

'It's a pleasure.'

Together they loaded all the pieces of wood into the back of Riley's truck, along with Findlaech's bicycle and then he drove him home.

After everything was unloaded Riley asked, 'Do you need help with that shelter, lad?'

'I think I've taken up enough of your time already, but thank you for your kind offer.'

He shook Riley's hand and thanked him again. Why had it taken him so long to realise just how nice people could be. He had always avoided them, not bothered to speak with anyone because of his dark moods, when all the time they were there and prepared to help. He couldn't help but feel guilty.

All his animals were extremely nosy and wanted to know what he was doing, in particular the goats that kept climbing on top of the woodpile. One of the sheep tried to follow but lost it's footing and fell back down.

'You're no mountain goat now, Fiona,' he said laughing. If only every day could be like today. He felt like a normal person not some lunatic locked away from the rest of the world. The problem was he never knew when the next episode would hit him. He knew he had to find a way of fighting the dark periods but that was easy to say when he felt normal.

He worked hard and managed to get the frame and the back of the shed finished before he heard the toot of a car horn. Instead of waiting for Findlaech to walk up the lane, Riley had come to pick him up. Findlaech was touched by this show of kindness.

'Thought you might be busy, lad, so I decided to save you some time.'

'Thank you, very thoughtful. I'll just go and wash my hands and then I'll be with you.'

Riley frowned. Wash his hands, he thought, very strange. He looked down at his own weather worn hands that were cracked and gnarled with grubby nails. He got out of the truck and followed Findlaech into the cottage.

'I think I might do the same,' he said holding out his hands.

Findlaech smiled. 'I think that's a good idea, Riley, we wouldn't want to take germs into the hospital now would we.'

'You know, lad, I would never have thought of that.' He shook his head in disbelief. Now who'd have believed it, he was learning manners from Findlaech Doyle.

The journey to the hospital, which Findlaech expected to be a solemn affair, was full of lighthearted banter. At first he struggled to join in, but as the miles slipped away so did his inhibitions and he found for the first time in years that he could hold a conversation without the embarrassment he had always felt. He wasn't sure why he suddenly felt so different and he could only put it down to Meabh and her big heart. For once he felt free, he didn't want to hide away, he genuinely wanted to see his new friend and make sure she was all right.

'Now how's that shelter coming along?' Riley asked.

'I've made the frame, put the back together and I think in a couple of days I will be ready to tackle the roof.'

'I've got a nice roll of roofing felt that's going begging and I won't take no for answer either. Once we know Meabh's all right I'll bring it down and we can work on it together.'

In all honesty, Riley had always wanted a son and Byrne had been the closest thing to one. When he died it hit him hard and to have the chance to get to know his brother after all this time was doing him the power of good. Women had always been a predominant feature in his life, which was great, but he did miss the company of a male to share jokes and chores with.

Riley was easy to talk to and Findlaech soon found he could relax in his company. He had been a fool; he did need people to help him get the most out of life. People – and his animals, of course.

When they arrived in the ward, Meabh was in the far corner next to the window. She had been propped up with a load of pillows and was sipping a cup of tea. She hadn't noticed them come in because she had headphones on listening to the hospital radio. In fact she didn't see them until they got right up to her bed.

Riley kissed her on the cheek and helped her remove her headphones.

'Oh, Findlaech, how lovely to see you,' she said, her face lighting up with the biggest of smiles.

'Hello Mrs Ceallaigh. Now what have you been up to?'

'Enough about me; how are you today, Findlaech?'

Findlaech could have cried. Here she was lying in a hospital bed recovering from a heart attack and she was worried about his health. These were two very special people and he felt guilty for not having realised it earlier in his life.

'I'm fine thanks to you,' he replied.

'Well, what did the doc have to say?' Riley added, desperate to know what the tests had shown.

'The doc says I have angina which was triggered by physical exertion due to my excessive weight. It's not serious at the moment but he did say it is a warning sign and that I could be at risk of a heart attack or stroke any time.'

'Oh, Mrs Ceallaigh, you see I said you needed to start taking it easy,' Riley said taking his wife's hand.

'Well, Doctor Donoghue did tell me to take more exercise.'

'Yes, but cleaning my whole house and doing my washing all in one day is too much,' Findlaech said.

'Now don't you go beating yourself up about that; it wasn't your fault and anyway I enjoyed helping you.'

'I made you that stew I promised.'

'Yes, he bought it round this morning, that's how he knew you weren't well.'

'I'm going to help you get well, Mrs Ceillaigh, so even on my very bad days I will have someone else to think about other than myself.'

'Findlaech, if you help yourself get well, then that will spur me on to lose some weight,' Meahb said smiling.

'Does that mean I have to go on a diet, too?' Riley said, his mouth turning downwards.

'Well, it wouldn't do you any harm now would it,' and she rubbed her hand over his protruding belly. 'Findlaech is going to teach me how to eat healthily and I am going to help him fight his "depressions". We made a pact.'

'I can see there has been a lot going on behind my back,' Riley said pretending to be offended, but then his face broke into an enormous smile and he patted Findlaech on the back. 'This all sounds splendid... splendid.'

The pact was renewed and now the pair had the full support of Meabh's husband.

They talked for the next hour about Findlaech's new shelter, the wood and roofing felt Riley had given him and also about how their daughter was getting on. Meabh explained how delighted they were when she got married but missed her terribly. Life was quiet around the farm without her laughter.

Meabh looked at Findlaech, took his hand, which is something that would have embarrassed him just a couple of days ago, and said, 'Findlaech you are welcome any time at the farm and you will be the son we never had.'

He went rather red and didn't know quite what to say. He felt his heart doing a little leap when he suddenly realised he actually had people who cared about him. Since the loss of his mother and brother he had felt nothing but loneliness and desolation, maybe this could be the kickstart he needed to get his life in order.

He decided an answer wasn't necessary but squeezed her hand to let her know he understood. He wanted to say she would be the mother he so desperately missed and Riley the father he had never known, but the words would not come. He hoped one day he would be able to tell them how he felt.

'You need to promise to call me when you have one of those bad days,' Meabh said not letting go of his hand. She knew this was hard for him, but he had come so far in twenty-four hours.

'I promise, but not until you get well.'

'Then you call me, lad,' Riley said patting him on the back. 'We will all be here for one another.'

'Now you two, I need my sleep, so be off with you,' she said playfully. 'I am allowed out tomorrow afternoon so you make sure you come and pick me up.'

'Back to her old bossy self already,' Riley said, getting off the chair and giving her another kiss, this time directly on the lips.

They waved as they walked down the ward, both looking back to give her their warmest smiles.

6 The Wayward Dog

Findlaech remained upbeat for the remainder of the day after visiting Meabh. He was full of energy, no headaches and no dark thoughts. He managed to put one side on the new shelter before it was time for supper and he made sure he washed up and put away every dish before he settled down to watch TV. He was going to turn over a new leaf. He had a lovely long soak in a nice hot bath before going to bed and lay reading a book until he felt tired enough to sleep. His brother wouldn't recognise him if he saw him now.

He was just about to turn out the lights when he heard a scratching at the door of the cottage. He climbed out of bed to see what the commotion was about. He assumed it was Ferris being too lazy to use the upstairs window and was about to reprimand him. However, when he opened the door he was shocked to see a scruffy little mongrel sitting on his doormat. Its fur was matted and full of burrs, its eyes barely open due to exhaustion.

'Hello. Where have you come from?'

He went to stroke the dog's head, but it shied away as if it was used to getting a beating. Findlaech backed away and went into the kitchen to fetch a scrap of cheese. When he returned the dog had moved a few steps and was now sitting inside but it was shaking all over.

'I won't hurt you. Here do you want something eat?'

Findlaech knelt down to make himself smaller and hopefully less of a threat. He held out his hand with the piece of cheese on his palm. The little dog sniffed the air. Slowly, Findlaech moved a little closer trying not to scare the animal. Again it sniffed the air but made no attempt to move or take the treat being offered.

'I don't even know if you are a girl or a boy,' Findlaech said keeping his voice calm. 'Come on you must be starving.'

It took almost twenty minutes of coaxing and talking to the little stray before he was close enough for the animal to take the cheese. Findlaech pretended to eat it himself in the hope that the dog would take the hint. Eventually his patience was rewarded when the dog could no longer stand the temptation and it leant forward and took the morsel out of his hand. It wolfed it down in seconds and started to salivate.

Findlaech had some cooked chicken in his fridge. He couldn't bear the thought of eating Matilda and Freda, but he did occasionally buy the odd capon from the market as his diet consisted of very little meat. He had some scraps left which he was going to add to a stew but he would much rather give them to the poor little stray that was in need of his help. The bones would still make some lovely tasty stock.

He got up slowly and to his surprise the little dog followed him into the kitchen. He got the chicken out of the fridge, picked the carcass clean, placed the scraps on an old saucer and then put it down on the floor along with a bowl of water.

The chicken was gone in seconds and the bowl drunk dry. Afterwards the dog lay down in front of the Aga enjoying the heat. Findlaech took the blanket off the chair where Ferris sometimes slept and spread it out on the floor. The dog immediately curled up on it and went to sleep.

'You can stay here tonight, but tomorrow I need to find out where you have come from. Someone could be out looking for you now.' Somehow he doubted his words, the dog was in too bad a state to have recently gone missing. It looked as though he had been fending for himself for quite some time. Satisfied that the little stray was comfortable for the night, Findlaech turned out all the lights and then headed back upstairs to bed.

He woke up at about two in the morning scratching like crazy. He couldn't imagine what was wrong with him, especially as he had bathed before going to bed. Then he realised the little stray must have come upstairs during the night, jumped on the bed and was sound asleep spooning to the shape of Findlaech's curved body. He didn't want to disturb it by putting the light on, but he really needed to find out what the source of the itching was.

As soon as the light shone onto the bedclothes he knew the answer. The little stray was riddled with fleas, most of which were making a meal of the pale skin on Findlaech's stomach.

'Right little fella, you are not going to like this, but if you want to share my bed I'm afraid it is a necessity. The dog opened one eye, gave him a suspicious look and then went back to sleep.

Findlaech ran the bath and went to fetch the large bottle of disinfectant that he used to douse the sheep and goats to keep away ticks and fleas. He put a capful into the warm water and then returned to the bedroom. He expected the dog to put up a fight, but it was so relieved to be in the warm and have a belly full of food that it put up little resistance.

It was a different kettle of fish when he put it in the bath though, it took all of Findlaech's strength just to keep it there and he got soaked in the process. He gave it a thoroughly good soaking, making sure the disinfectant got right through to its skin. He had had the forethought to bring a comb and little by little he managed to comb out most of the knots and decided he would cut the really bad ones out later. The water was black by the time he had finished and the dog unrecognisable.

He towelled it as dry as he could and then went back to the bedroom to strip his bed of the flea-ridden covers. He sprayed the mattress and put all the bedding into his old twin-tub ready to wash tomorrow. Because his bed was damp, he took an old eiderdown out of the airing cupboard and made up a bed on the sofa for the rest of the night.

He was glad the old cottage had no carpets; at least he didn't have to worry about infestation in anything else. He was just about to lie down when he remembered the blanket he had put down in front of the Aga; that would need a wash too. He checked the sofa to make sure no fleas had made their way up there and, once satisfied, he lay down and fell asleep instantly.

He slept fairly well until about seven-thirty when he got up to make himself his first cup of tea. The mutt had curled up in front of the Aga for the rest of the night, obviously deciding there was not enough room on the sofa for the two of them. He put the kettle on and then called the dog to see if it needed to go outside. It obediently got up and went out into the yard, did its business and then turned round and came back inside. Findlaech had half expected it to run away after what it had been through last night, but no it had decided this was home and this was where it was going to stay.

He studied the little dog now it was clean. He had discovered it was a boy during the bathing debacle. Most of its fur was white with one black patch over his left eye, one on his back near its tail and then a couple of brown marks down his front legs. The dog really was a Heinz 57, although he thought he could see a bit of collie in it by the shape of his head.

'Right you need a name, I can't keep calling you 'dog'. I know, Conan, that's quite apt because it means little wolf. You came to me in the night just like a wolf prowling for its prey.'

At breakfast Conan sat at the foot of the table waiting for food. There was no chicken left so he had to make do with scrambled eggs with some of the leftover sourdough broken up into it. Just as before the little dog wolfed it down in no time and then sat wagging its tail.

Findlaech bent down and stroked its back. Findlaech knew some dogs feel threatened when you stroke their head, so he started lower down until he gained its confidence. He had been so busy tending to the dog and the infestation in the night he hadn't had time to think whether he had one of his 'depressions' or not. His head was clear, he felt positive and somehow he knew he was going to have another good day.

After breakfast, Findlaech got dressed and told Conan that he was going out to feed the animals and continue building the shelter. Conan cocked his head to one side as if listening and even wagged his tail. When Findlaech went out into the yard the little dog followed and it seemed wherever he went his new buddy was going to stick to him like glue. While he was busy working on the shelter, the dog curled up in the sunshine waiting patiently.

Findlaech was up a ladder hammering a board to the side of the shelter when he heard the commotion. He looked down to find Conan chasing Matilda and Freda who were squawking and flapping their wings trying to put their pursuer off. The dog was barking and when the two chickens ran into the kitchen and he had them cornered, the squawks turned into high-pitched squeals. Findlaech got down from the ladder as fast as he could and ran into the kitchen just in time to stop Freda from becoming tonight's dinner.

'No!' he yelled, grabbing Conan by the scruff of his neck. 'That's just not on!'

He picked the dog up, put it under his armpit and headed off towards the old shelter where he knew he had a ball of baling twine. He cut a piece off using his penknife, not letting go of the dog, and tied it around his neck and then onto a fence post so that he could not do any more chasing.

'If you want to live here, then you have to learn to get on with the rest of the family and that includes the chickens and geese.'

Conan did not like being tied up at all and he struggled and struggled. The string got tighter and tighter around his neck until Findlaech was worried that it would cut into his skin. He decided it would be safer to shut him in the kitchen for the time being until he could get a proper collar and lead for him.

So for the rest of the afternoon Conan was shut away while Findlaech continued with his building project. The feirme returned to peace and quiet.

It had seemed like quite a good idea at the time, but when Findlaech went in later that afternoon to start getting tea ready he discovered it had been a very bad idea. The remains of his wellington boots were all over the kitchen floor, Conan had peed on his slippers and even left him another nice present under the table. Inside he was smiling but he wasn't going to show it to the dog, so he growled to show his disapproval.

'Oh Conan, you have a lot to learn. Now out you go while I clear up and no chasing the animals.'

Once again the floor had a liberal dousing of hot water and disinfectant, his slippers had to go in the washing machine and what was left of his boots went in the bin. Conan was starting to test his patience but he wasn't prepared to give up on him yet.

He went back outside into the yard to make sure the dog was behaving himself. He needn't have worried; he was about to be taught a lesson. Goliath, Findlaech's oversized billy goat had caught Conan's attention and he thought it would be a good idea to chase him. Findlaech was about to reprimand the little dog, but then thought better of it. He knew Goliath could look after himself and this might just be the lesson the dog needed. Sure enough, at first Goliath just ran through the open gate into the meadow with Conan in hot pursuit. Unhappy with the barking, Goliath turned, put his head down, and stamped his front hoof on the ground. Conan, who obviously had no idea about goats and that this was a warning, carried on and ran up to him still barking. Goliath, who had had enough by this time, put his head down, pushing his enormous curved horns towards Conan. Conan didn't back off, which was a big mistake. Suddenly the little mutt was flying through the air, its tail and ears flying in the wind. He let out quite a squeal as he hit the ground and then noticed that the goat was coming in for a second bout. Conan got to his feet as quickly as he could, ran for all he was worth towards the yard and straight through the door of the cottage where Findlaech was standing.

'Hopefully that has taught you a lesson, Conan. You do not mess with the animals on my feirme. If you want to stay here you need to learn to abide by the rules.'

The dog skulked under the table with his tail between his legs, a very pitiful sight. That was the first day of life with a wayward dog and Findlaech wondered what tomorrow would bring. Life was hard enough without bringing another animal into the equation, but he found it impossible to turn his back on something that was so needy.

'OK, one more chance, Conan. If you don't mend your ways, you hear me, you will be out that door and have to go back to fending for yourself.'

Conan cocked his head to one side, listening intently to what his new master had to say.

'You know what, I believe you know exactly what I am saying.'

7 Conan to the Rescue

The sun shone through the bedroom window penetrating the thin fabric of the floral curtains that hung in Findlaech's bedroom. He was not one for floral or chintzy material, but he had been too lazy to replace them after the death of his mother. The brightness woke him and as soon as he opened one eye he knew it was going to be a black day.

'No! No! Not again!' he cried out loud.

There were so many chores to be done, but even the bright sunlight trying to tempt him out of bed was not enough to lift his spirits. Everything seemed hopeless. Why on earth had he thought he had turned a corner? Why did he believe that someone could help him? Nobody could help him, he was afflicted with 'the depressions' and it was obvious they were not going away.

Since the bathing episode in the middle of the night Conan had decided it was safer to sleep downstairs on his blanket, enjoying the warmth from the Aga. However, when he heard his master calling out in obvious pain, he scampered up the stairs, pushed the door open by jumping against it and then leapt onto the bed.

'Not now Conan, I'm not in the mood.'

Aware that his master was behaving differently, the little dog edged his way up the bed keeping down low on his tummy. Even when Findlaech pushed him away he didn't give up. He just carried on creeping closer and closer to his master's face until he was within reach to give him a lick on the end of his nose. Pleased with himself, Conan sat up and started to wag his tail.

Yesterday this would have got a reaction, but today he was failing to get his master's attention. He knew something wasn't right. His first instinct was not to run away but to persevere until he got some kind of response. He tried barking, jumping off the bed and running to the door. He did this several times, but each time Findlaech just buried his head in his pillow allowing the darkness to take him.

Today life really didn't seem worth living and no matter how many times he told himself his animals needed him, he could not break through the wall of dark mist penetrating his thoughts. He turned his head and stared at the glass of water standing on the bedside table. The sun caught in the glass making the water look even more enticing. He slowly pulled the drawer open, took out the pills that the doctor had left him, pushed down on the cap and turned it. The little blue pills were calling to him, each one encouraging him to swallow it to make the pain go away. Instead of taking just the two as prescribed, he emptied the entire bottle into his hand, tipping them into his mouth, using the water to help them go down.

He lay down on his back this time, resting his head on the pillow. Tears flowed from his eyes, down the sides of his face, soaking the pillow. Today he had given up hope of ever feeling normal despite the best efforts of Meabh and Riley. Every day he knew he risked waking up feeling like this and he couldn't take it any longer. He didn't want to be a burden. Nobody else mattered, nothing else mattered, all he wanted was to sink into oblivion and it all to end. He closed his eyes and let the wonderful feeling of oblivion envelop him.

Conan had watched his master carefully; at first believing he was getting something for him to eat out of the drawer. He cocked his head to the side as Findlaech swallowed the little blue pills and then as he sank into a deep sleep alarm bells started ringing inside the little dog's brain. He jumped on and off the bed barking incessantly, trying to bring his master out of his induced sleep. He even jumped on and off his stomach, but got no reaction whatsoever. Something told the little dog his master needed help and it was pure instinct that made him leave the cottage and run down the lane. It had been a real struggle to get his body through the flap in the door that gave Matilda and Freda access to the kitchen, but he wriggled and wriggled until he managed to get outside.

With his nose to the ground he followed Findlaech's scent all along the stony path, across the lane that bordered their feirme and the neighbouring property. He followed the scent right up the path until he came to the old door with green peeling paint. He had no idea who lived there, but he did know he had to get their attention. He jumped up and down scratching the door with his long claws whilst barking as loudly as he possibly could.

His perseverance paid off and eventually the door opened.

'Now what do you think you are doing?' Meabh said as she watched the strange little dog doing somersaults and barking like crazy.

'Da, will you come here and see this crazy dog,' she called out.

Riley, who was still in the process of getting dressed, came to the door with his braces over one shoulder and his work trousers barely pulled up to his waist.

'Crazy is the right word for that one,' he said. 'What on earth do you suppose he is doing?'

'I've no idea, but he keeps jumping up, barking and then running back down the path.'

'Do you know who he belongs to?' Riley asked his wife.

'No, no idea. I've never seen him around these parts before.'

Conan was getting frustrated; these people didn't seem to understand what he wanted. In desperation he ran up to Meabh, jumped up and pulled on the bottom of her apron. It was on his third attempt that Meabh turned to her husband and said, 'Do you know Da, I think this little dog is trying to tell us something. He wants us to follow him.'

'Aw, Ma, are you sure?'

'Yes, I'm certain. He is being so persistent I think someone is in trouble. Grab your boots we need to see where he takes us.'

Riley pulled up his trousers, hooked the other strap of his braces over his shoulder, put on his big work boots and cap and then followed his wife down the garden path and across the lane.

Conan ran on ahead, stopping every so often to look back, making sure they were following him.

'He's taking us down to Findlaech's place,' Meabh said extremely out of breath from the exertion.

'Do you think you should be running in your state of health?' Riley asked her, a little out of breath himself. 'You've only just come out of hospital and I certainly don't want to have to take you back.'

'Aw, stop your fussing. Findlaech is in trouble and he needs us,' she said dismissing him with a wave of her hand.

Once they arrived at the cottage, Conan again jumped up and down trying to push the door open.

'All right, all right, we are coming,' Meabh said, getting to the front door as fast as her swollen legs would carry her.

She turned the handle and immediately made her way upstairs, followed by her husband who by this time was very red in the face and sweating profusely. She instinctively went straight to the bedroom only to find Conan already on the bed and pawing at Findlaech's chest.

'Off, off,' Meabh said, pushing the little dog off the bed.

She felt Findlaech's pulse, which was extremely weak, and told Riley to call for an ambulance straight away. It was then she noticed the empty bottle of pills lying on the bedside table.

The blood drained from her face and she thought she was going to faint.

'No, no, Findlaech, we made a pact. Nothing is that bad that you have to take your own life.' She laid her head on his chest and started sobbing her heart out.

Riley, who had been downstairs to use the phone, had returned by this time and it broke his heart to see his wife so distressed.

'Now, now, Ma, don't be getting yourself so upset. This isn't good for you.'

'But . . . but . . . but I promised to be there for him and I wasn't when he needed me most,' she sobbed.

Riley sat down on the chair in the corner of the room and allowed a few tears of his own to slide down his cheeks. It was perfectly true, no one had ever tried to understand Findlaech, but he had got to know him a little better in the last couple of days and had seen him in a different light. He felt sad that perhaps their help had come a little too late.

It seemed an age before the ambulance arrived. The room had been deathly quiet with Meabh still sitting on the bed holding Findlaech's hand, Conan lying up by his head on the pillow and Riley deep in thought. The paramedics checked for his vital signs, carried him downstairs on a stretcher and took the empty pill bottle with them so they could tell the doctors at Sligo General Hospital exactly what he had taken.

'Will he be all right?' Meabh asked, still stunned by what had happened.

'It's hard to say at the moment Mrs Ceallaigh, but as you told us he has no next of kin you are welcome to accompany him in the ambulance.'

This brought a smile to her face.

'Really?' she asked.

'Yes, really. He will need a friendly face if he comes round.'

Meabh didn't like the sound of the word *if* she would have preferred it if they had said *when*. She looked at her husband to see if he was happy for her to go. Riley just nodded and told her he would go and get the truck and meet her there.

The ride took almost an hour, allowing for traffic on The Mall. Meabh held Findlaech's hand all the way and kept talking to him while the paramedics fixed an oxygen mask to his face and put a drip in his arm. She watched as the clear fluid dripped slowly down the tube and into the canula in his vein.

Meabh was a good Catholic woman and in between chatting she said her own little prayer asking for Findlaech to be saved. She wasn't sure why she felt such an affinity with the young man, but she knew if she lost him it would somehow be like losing a son. It was strange how they had become so close in a matter of days, but he had most definitely found a place in her heart.

Riley and Meabh had always wanted a second child, but it wasn't to be. It had hit them hard when the doctors told her she would be unable to bear any more children, but their bond as husband and wife was unbreakable. They spoilt Niamh, perhaps a little too much, but they both had something missing – a son. When Byrne died it was so painful, he had become the son they didn't have, and now there was a chance his brother would go the same way.

When they arrived at A&E, it was a bustle of activity and Meabh was asked to go and sit in the waiting room. They promised to call her as soon as they had any news. She looked around her at all the people who were waiting to be seen, some obviously in a lot of discomfort, and she vowed she would do everything in her power to lose weight and get healthy. She would do it for Riley, she would do it for Findlaech, but most of all she would do it for herself. She was fed up with being out of breath, lugging her large body around, so instead of getting herself a hot chocolate drink to comfort her she chose water instead.

'Are you all right Meabh?' a voice said behind her.

She turned to see Riley and she patted the seat beside her.

'Guess who followed me back home and jumped in the cab of the truck as soon as I opened the door?'

Meabh frowned in thought, 'Ah, the wee doggie.'

Riley nodded.

'Where is he now?'

'Still sitting in the cab, he seemed to understand that he couldn't come in. That's some intelligent dog.'

'I didn't know Findlaech had a dog?' Meabh said. 'It wasn't around when I was last over there.'

'Well, I guess we will solve the puzzle when he comes round,' Riley said putting an arm round his wife's shoulders.

'I'm so glad you said *when*, Riley, I don't think I could bear it if you said *if* as well.'

'Oh, it's most definitely *when*, Ma, I can feel it in me bones.'

'Aw, Riley, what on earth would I do without you,' and she gave him a big kiss right in front of everyone, causing Riley to blush and look around anxiously.

It was another hour and ten minutes before a nurse came to fetch them.

'Mr and Mrs Ceallaigh, I believe you came in with Findlaech Doyle? He is over the worst. We have pumped his stomach and also given him some medication to reverse the effects of the overdose, which means he should be awake by now, only he doesn't seem to be responding. Perhaps you would like to come up and talk to him, see if you can get any response.'

'Oh, yes...' she thought for a couple of seconds before continuing, '...we will do anything if you think it will help.'

They followed the nurse to the end of the corridor where she told them to take the lift to the second floor.

Just like downstairs, the second floor was a mass of corridors and doors.

'Do you know where we'll be finding Findlaech Doyle?' she asked a nurse hurrying down the corridor pushing a trolley full of medications.

'Go and check at reception down the end there, they'll be able to help you.'

They made their way down the pristine corridor and waited until the nurse manning the station had finished on the phone.

'Can I help you?' she said, her face full of smiles.

'We're looking for Findlaech Doyle,' Meabh said, returning her smile. She saw the dark circles under the nurse's eyes and how her forehead was etched with worry lines. She admired anyone who had the stomach to do such a demanding job.

The nurse looked at her computer screen, then told them he had been put in room number eleven. 'Turn left down there,' she said pointing, 'then right and you'll see the door right in front of you. Press the buzzer above the bed if you need anything.'

'Thank you nurse, that's very helpful,' Meabh said, taking Riley's arm.

They opened the door to room eleven slowly and tried not to make too much noise with their shoes on the polished floor. Findlaech was a sorry sight, almost as white as the sheets he lay on, and breathing with the help of a ventilator.

'Oh, Da, look at him,' Meabh said walking up to the side of the bed.

Riley put a couple of chairs either side of the bed and they sat down with heavy hearts.

'They said we should talk to him. What do you think we should say?' Riley asked in a whisper.

'I don't think we need to whisper, that's for sure. We need to be upbeat and talk about everyday things. Anything to try and get his attention.'

Meabh took Findlaech's hand and held it in hers, stroking his skin with her thumb.

'You never told me you had a wee dog, Findlaech. Now what do you call him? You know he was the one who saved you.'

Meabh talked and talked about anything that came into her head; sometimes imagining she could see a flicker of his eyelids or a slight movement in his fingers. After a full hour of talking her voice was getting croaky and she hadn't even noticed that her husband had gone out and come back with two steaming teas in polystyrene cups.

'Here you are, Ma, I thought you could do with one of these.'

'Riley, I don't seem to be getting through to him. You know what I think, you should go down and get that wee doggie and bring him up here. Perhaps that will shake him out of the doldrums.'

'I think you might be right, Ma, but do you think they would allow a dog in a hospital. Isn't it a bit unhygienic.'

'They said we should do anything to get him to respond, didn't they. So why don't you go down and get him. Hide him under your coat and that way no one will know he is here.'

Riley was not sure about her hare-brained scheme, but once Meabh had her mind set on something there was no shifting her.

'If you think it will help,' he said reluctantly.

'I do, Da, so off with you.'

It was raining cats and dogs by the time Riley reached the truck. The little dog was sitting patiently on the front seat where he had left him.

'Now I need you to behave yourself, you understand little fella. I've got to try and sneak you in without them nurses and doctors spotting you first.'

As if Conan understood every word, he lay down flat on his tummy and allowed Riley to wrap his jacket around him. He tucked him under his arm and told him to keep very still.

By the time they reached the main doors Riley was soaked through to the skin, but had managed to keep the little dog covered for the most part. He held him close to his body and managed miraculously to sneak him up to the second floor and into room eleven without too much difficulty.

Meabh looked over her shoulder as the door opened.

'Aw, well done, Da. I had every faith in you.'

Riley uncovered the dog and placed him on the bed, leaving big puddles on the floor as the water dripped off his clothing. The dog immediately started to wag his tail and jumped onto Findlaech's chest. When he didn't get a response, he did it again and again, eventually walking up to his face and giving it a big, wet lick.

He watched his master's face and when he saw no sign of response he barked loudly and jumped on him for the umpteenth time.

'Shhh, you'll get the nurses running in here in a minute,' Riley said nervously. 'It's not working, Ma, I think I'd better take him back downstairs.'

Meabh wanted to give him another five minutes, but knew

it was very unlikely they would remain undiscovered for much longer. She was just about to agree with her husband when she heard a moan. She turned back quickly towards the bed only to see Findlaech had his eyes open and was staring right into the little dog's face. Conan got really excited at getting a reaction and started licking every available bit of skin.

'That's enough little doggie, that's enough,' Riley said, lifting him off the bed and covering him once again with his jacket.

'Quick make a run for it, Da, while I ring the buzzer. I knew that little dog could work his magic.'

Meabh waited until the coast was clear and then pressed the little red buzzer above Findlaech's bed. It seemed just seconds later that a nurse ran into the room.

'He's awake,' Meabh said with a big smile. 'He wants to talk but can't with that tube down his throat. Can it come out?'

'I'll just check with his doctor. I'll be back in a sec.'

Half an hour later, Findlaech was propped up in bed, all the tubes having been removed.

'You can go back in now Mrs Ceallaigh, only remember he'll be very tired so take it easy.'

'Oh thank you, nurse, thank you,' she said excitedly.

She almost ran back into room eleven and scuttled over to the bed. Findlaech had a lot more colour in his cheeks, but his eyes told her he was not in a good place.

'Oh, Findlaech, you had us worried there,' she said taking his hand.

He said nothing, but the tears had started to flow and his body shook with the immensity of the sobs.

Meabh held him in her arms until the crying stopped.

'I thought we had a pact, young man,' she reprimanded. 'If I can't trust you then I am going to have to come and stay at your place.'

'I'm sorry,' was all he managed to say.

'And so I should think so, what were you thinking.'

'That's just it, Meabh, I wasn't thinking, I didn't want to think anymore. I don't want to wake up not knowing whether it is going to be a good day or a bad day.'

'But listen son, aren't the good days worth it. Just think how happy you were yesterday.'

He didn't say anything for quite a while.

'How did you find me?' he asked.

'It was that wee dog of yours. He came and got us.'

'He did?'

'Yes, and he was very persistent. He cares an awful lot about you. We didn't know you had a dog by the way.'

'I didn't. He just turned up on my doorstep a couple of days ago and seemed to adopt me.'

'And what's his name. I can't keep calling him 'dog'?'

'It's Conan. I can't believe he actually came to fetch you. How on earth did he know where to go?'

'I can't answer that I'm afraid, but he certainly is one very special little dog.'

'He's been quite a bit of bother, actually, but now I am starting to see him in a different light. I was going to take him to the pound, but now how on earth could I let him go.'

'He'll be a grand companion for you, Findlaech. I definitely think you should keep him. Now listen, and I don't want you moaning at me. Before you leave this hospital I am going to ask for you to see a special doctor, a doctor who knows all about these here depressions. You can't do this on your own any more, but you already know that.'

'No, Meabh, I'll not be talking to any special doctor. You know they will think I am mad and put me in a place where mad people go. I would rather be dead than have to go in a place like that.' He put his head in his hands and cried, deep heart-wrenching sobs.

'Don't be silly. You're not in the slightest bit mad; it's just that your brain doesn't want to function properly some days. These special doctors know all about these type of things and they will be able to help you. Now what do you say, we made a pact?'

Findlaech looked down at the pale blue bedspread and fiddled with a loose piece of thread. He knew he needed help but could he really talk to someone he didn't know? He realised just how much Meabh and Riley cared for him, it was obvious, and now the little dog seemed to have formed a bond as well. Didn't they deserve for him to get better?

He eventually managed to look Meabh in the eyes.

'I will do this for you and for Riley and now it seems for Conan, too. I am not sure it will help but I know I can't go on like this.'

'Now that's the ticket, Findlaech, I knew you would see the sense in what I said.'

8 Gaffer Tape to the Rescue

Findlaech was allowed to go home after forty-eight hours of further observation. There was one condition to his release, however, that he agreed to come back in a week's time and talk to the psychiatrist. The doctor's name was O'Mahony and Findlaech had found him easy to talk to when he did his ward rounds.

Meabh had stayed at Findlaech's to keep an eye on the animals and when Riley dropped him back home his place was warm, spotless and the smell of vegetable curry made him salivate.

'Oh, you shouldn't have done all this Meabh,' he said feeling somewhat embarrassed that he had caused such an upheaval in the Ceallaigh's lives.

'Oh, now don't you be worrying about us, Findlaech, the important thing is that we get you better,' Meabh said taking his coat and hanging it on the hook behind the front door.

She filled two huge bowls with curry and brown rice and a smaller one for herself and set them on the table.

'Now get that down you, it'll make you feel like a new man,' she said breaking into a broad smile.

'And me, I hope, because Meabh could certainly do with a new man,' Riley said laughing.

'Oh, away with you, I can't be doing with any new man, you are enough of a man for me.'

Findlaech listened to the friendly banter between the two people who had become so important to him. He wasn't in the right frame of mind to join in as yet, but their jovial manner was starting to make him feel better. He ate, listened to the chatter and realised he was actually enjoying the company.

Once they had eaten and all the dishes had been washed and put away, they sat down in the small lounge in front of an open fire with steaming cups of coffee.

Meabh was a little loath to bring up the topic of doctors, but she needed to know if he had kept his promise.

'Did you manage to make an appointment to see a doctor, Findlaech?' she asked tentatively.

'Aye, Meabh, I surely did.'

He paused while he took a sip of his coffee.

'And . . . more information please?' she pushed him.

'Aw, Ma, stop yer blatherin', poor lad has only just stepped foot in the front door.'

'I'll no rest until I know he is taking care of hisself.'

'It's all right, I am seeing a doctor O'Mahony next week. He explained to me that I was suffering from something called Bipolar and that I would need cognitive behavioural therapy and most definitely medication.'

'You mean you haven't got "the depressions"?' Meabh said sounding a little shocked.

'I believe, Meabh, that's the medical term for them.'

'Well I never. Sounds like something you'd find in the Arctic,' Riley said following it with a belly laugh.

'Very funny, Da, enough of your silly jokes.'

Then they both turned in unison because Findlaech had tears running down his cheeks, not from depression this time, but because Riley had made him laugh.

'Oh, Riley, you are funny. What would I do without you two?' Findlaech said once the laughter had subsided. It made him realise just how lonely he had been.

'Well, Findlaech, you won't have to do without us. We had a long talk while you were in the hospital and we decided until you get yourself back on your feet we are coming to stay here...'

Findlaech put his hands up to stop her. 'And what about your own feirme, who would look after that for you?'

'It's all sorted, lad,' Riley said leaning forward and placing his elbows on his knees. 'My cousin is coming over from Tobercurry to mind the place. He thinks it's a grand idea because he hates his job in the factory and has always dreamed of having his own feirme.'

'I can't let you do this. It's just too disruptive for you,' he said, pushing himself backwards into the chair.

'You can and it's not. It's what we want to do Findlaech,' Meabh said trying to get the young man to look her in the eye.

Findlaech suddenly stood up and walked to the other side of the room.

'No, Meabh. I won't have it. I will not be a burden on anyone,' and he stormed out of the room with Conan grabbing at the bottom of his trousers trying to prevent him from leaving.

Riley immediately stood up and went to follow him, but Meabh put a gentle hand on his arm and shook her head. 'He needs a bit of space, leave him be.'

Findlaech went and stood outside his partially finished shelter and lit up a cigarette. He didn't understand why he was feeling angry when all they were trying to do was help.

He had always found it hard to accept help since his mother died. Life had been easier on his own because he hadn't had to think, or cope with the emotions involved with being around other people. Was now the time he should change? He knew it would be hard to accept help but he knew he couldn't do it on his own. He was too scared he would try to take his own life the next time he had a bad day.

Meabh left him to his own thoughts for about ten minutes, before grabbing her jacket and following him out into the garden. She could see the glow of the cigarette and the smoke drifting in the breeze, so she knew where he was. The wind had a bite to it now that summer was over and she pulled her knitted jacket round her ample bosom.

'Please don't be angry, Findlaech. You have become like a son to us and we are doing this because we care not because we feel obliged.'

She lifted his chin gently with her hand until he had to look her in the eye.

'Please, Findlaech, please let us help you. It will be so nice having someone to look after again. I miss Niamh so much now she has moved out.'

Findlaech saw the imploring look in her eyes. It was not a look of sympathy; he could see it was genuine and that this charming woman actually cared for him. He was not one to show his emotions but Meabh had found a place in his heart and he held her in a hug and whispered 'thank you' in her ear.

'Should I have reason to be jealous?' Riley said walking up to the pair.

'Only jealous because I am the one to be hugging our new

found son,' Meabh said with a tear in her eye, but there was a warm feeling in her heart that had been missing for quite some time.

'It's all settled then?' Riley asked hopefully.

Meabh looked at Findlaech.

'It's all settled,' Findlaech said shaking Riley's hand.

'Don't I get a hug too?'

'Do men do that kind of thing?' Findlaech asked.

'They most definitely do in our house.'

The deal was made and Findlaech suddenly felt like a weight had been lifted from his shoulders.

'You know what, I think a lovely cup of hot chocolate and then bed,' Meabh said putting a saucepan of milk on top of the Aga.

Findlaech slept soundly that night in the comfort of his own bed. Conan was spooning in his curved body and the gentle rhythm of his breathing had rocked him to sleep. He did feel better knowing there was someone in the house and the next morning he knew it was going to be one of his 'up' days. He climbed out of bed ready for what the day might throw at him.

It was a beautiful autumn day with a light breeze and they discussed over breakfast their chores for the day.

'I would really like to get the shelter finished before the worst of winter sets in,' Findlaech said. 'I'd appreciate your experience with that.'

Riley was delighted and slapped him on his back. 'It'll be a real pleasure, son.'

They worked well together, saying very little, but in tune

with one another's needs. They passed tools to each other, measured pieces of wood and sorted through the assortment of nails and screws Riley had fetched from his own workshop.

Meabh sat outside the front door with a rug over her knees working wool through the spinning wheel. The sun had given a beautiful pink tinge to her cheeks and Riley didn't think he had seen his wife so happy since their daughter left home. He took a deep sigh and was thankful for the life they had been blessed with.

It was almost four o'clock and the sun was sinking behind the mountain by the time they were satisfied the shelter was fit for its purpose. Meabh had gone in an hour earlier to start supper and Riley and Findlaech were about to go off for a pint of Guinness when Conan started running around like a mad thing and barking at something in the distance.

'What do you think is wrong with him?' Findlaech asked.

'Well, this is exactly how he was acting when he came to fetch us, so I don't think we should ignore him.'

The dog was bouncing up and down trying to get them to open the gate that led out to the paddocks. It was then that Findlaech realised his nanny goat was missing. Goliath was pawing the ground and trumpeting in an alarming way.

Findlaech grabbed a ball of twine, a torch, a headlamp and his penknife and then opened the gate. Conan went charging off across the paddock in the direction of the mountain.

'You go ahead, son, I'll never keep up with your pace. Keep shining the flashlight in my direction then I'll know how to find you.'

He didn't need telling twice and Findlaech started running

after Conan yelling for him to wait. When he reached the foot of the mountain he could hear the goat's bleating which Findlaech immediately recognised as a sound of distress. Conan was standing on a ledge of rock looking across a quite substantial crevasse to a ridge on the far side. Snowy was balanced on the ridge unable to go either up or down, her bright white coat now shining as the moon made its presence known in the night sky.

'Stay still, Snowy, we'll get you down,' Findlaech said trying to keep his own voice calm.

He waved his torch back across the meadow and saw the flash of Riley's light as he made his way towards him.

Conan had managed to work his way down the crevasse and was scaling his way up the other side. Findlaech and Riley watched in fascination as the little dog slid and then regained his footing until he had made it onto the ridge. He sat just in front of Snowy and then barked across to Findlaech.

'I told you that's some clever little dog,' Riley said. 'Look, he's keeping the goat calm and making sure she doesn't try and jump.'

'What do you think we should do Riley?' Findlaech asked, knowing that with age came wisdom and experience.

'What did you bring with you?'

'A ball of twine, my penknife and . . .' he scrabbled around in his deep jacket pockets for few seconds '. . . a roll of gaffer tape. Not that gaffer tape will be much help in this situation.'

'I don't know, Findlaech, it might just. You can make all sorts of things out of gaffer tape.'

'What were you thinking?' Riley asked, raising one eyebrow in surprise.

'What I was thinking, son, was that we could fashion some sort of harness out of the twine and the gaffer tape and hopefully you could get across to the ridge, fasten it around the goat and we could lower her to safety.'

Findlaech was not convinced, it sounded like a bit of a far-fetched scheme to him. However, he didn't want to undermine Riley's suggestion and just nodded in agreement.

'Give me the twine and gaffer tape, son.'

Findlaech passed them over, along with his knife, and watched in awe as his mentor cut and tied, cut and tied, and, when he was happy that he had fashioned a reasonable harness, covered it all in gaffer tape to make it as secure as possible. Finally, he attached several thickness of twine to make a long rope and secured those with the gaffer tape also. He tied the new piece of rope to the back of the harness and handed the whole contraption over to Findlaech.

The final piece of the rescue equipment was another rope fashioned out of the twine and gaffer tape, which Riley then tied round Findlaech's waist. Findlaech finished the ensemble by putting the headlamp on his forehead, so he could see where he was going.

'Right, son, you now need to try and get over to that ridge without hurting yourself.'

'Right, easier said than done, I would imagine.'

'You'll be fine, you're young. I'm going to tie this end of the rope around that rock and then I'll take up the slack while you climb down.'

They placed both their flashlights on the ground so that it lit up the rock face which, with the headlamp in place, gave

Findlaech just enough light to see where he was going.

Findlaech placed the makeshift harness over his shoulder, tying the rope round his waist so as not to lose it or trip over any loose ends. He then made his way gingerly down the slope, slipping and sliding as the loose scree came away under his feet. Every so often he managed to get a foothold on a piece of firm rock or a small shrub growing out of the rock. He eventually made his way to the bottom and then looked up towards the ridge. It was a daunting task and seemed a lot further up than when he had looked from the other side.

Riley was shouting words of encouragement from the top and with the addition of Conan's barking and Snowy's incessant bleating it gave him enough incentive to attempt the ascent. To get a bit of momentum he climbed partially back up the hill he had just descended and then ran for all his might at the rock face in front of him, grabbing hold of a clump of grass and a piece of rock to get his first handholds. Little by little he made some headway up the rock face until his head appeared over the rim and he could see the animals' feet. As soon as his shoulders were over the edge of the ridge, Conan grabbed Findlaech's jacket and pulled with all his might. Findlaech's foot slipped a couple of times, but eventually he managed to get a good footing and he heaved himself over the edge. He lay breathless on the ridge, sweating profusely from the effort and relieved to have made it. All he had to do now was get down again!

He started shaking, initially believing it was from all the exertion, but then realised it was because it bought back bad memories of the night his mother died. His whole body was quivering and then the tears came as it all came flooding back.

Riley called over to see if he was all right and it took him a few seconds to pull himself together. He called back that he had made it safely and then turned to his dog.

'Thank you, Conan, you are a star,' he said patting the little dog's head. Conan was delighted with the attention he was receiving and wagged his little tail so hard his bottom wiggled which made Findlaech laugh. Snowy, who had been quite surprised to see Findlaech appear over the ridge, had stopped bleating and now put her head forward to receive a stroke as well.

'Now you need to remain calm while I fix this harness to you, Snowy,' he said giving her words of encouragement. 'You do understand we are trying to help you, don't you?'

She butted him with her head, nearly causing him to lose his balance.

He took the harness off his shoulder, untied the rope from his waist, making sure to keep the second rope in place so that Riley could help pull him up again. Snowy seemed to understand that he was helping her and she stood perfectly still while he put the harness over her head and then managed to get each of her front legs through the appropriate gaps. Once he was happy it was secure, he tied the far end of the rope to a firm piece of rock, then gradually started to lower her down. He made sure he had his feet planted firmly behind a rock to give him purchase and gradually let the rope out. Snowy started bleating again on her descent, Conan started whining, but they were making progress. Findlaech was just glad it wasn't Goliath on the other end, now that would have been a completely different story.

Riley kept Findlaech informed as to how much further he needed to lower her because there was no way Findlaech could move from his position at the back of the ridge.

'Just a couple more feet, son, and she'll be on solid ground,' he called in encouragement.

Findlaech knew when Snowy had reached the bottom because there was no more weight on the end of the rope, which, by the way, had held out superbly despite only being made of twine and gaffer tape. Once he was happy she was safe, he untied the rope from the rock and let it fall into the crevasse. He would throw it up to Riley once he had made his way down.

Now he had the daunting task of climbing back down, something he really wasn't looking forward to, especially as he had no rope to break his fall. He was just about to put his leg over the edge when Conan barked at him and started running off to his left. Findlaech followed him, intrigued by his behaviour. Conan had discovered a deep fissure between the rocks, on the other side of which was a much easier descent.

'Wait, Conan, I need to tell Riley where we are going and I have to untie this rope,' he called after the dog, which had already bounded on ahead.

Findlaech went back to the ridge and called across to Riley to tell him what he was about to do.

'Okay, lad, but take care,' he called back in the darkness.

Findlaech untied the rope from his waist and dropped it down into the crevasse. Then he struggled like crazy to get his body through the narrow fissure. At one point he was totally stuck and didn't know what to do. Conan just stood on the other side barking at him, encouraging him to try again. He wriggled and wriggled, trying to get through the crack and eventually he managed to get one shoulder through and then finally the other. He put his hands on the ground and pulled as hard as he could to get his hips and legs through to the other side. After a lot of grunting and groaning, and encouraging barks from Conan, Findlaech made it through. The path down had a lot of loose rocks, but it was a much easier descent and most probably the way Snowy had found her way up to the ledge in the first place.

It took about ten minutes to make their way to the grassy track at the bottom of the crevasse where Snowy was happily chewing away on some alpine plants.

'I'm going to take her back the other way,' Findlaech called up to Riley. 'It's a long way round but it will be a lot safer than trying to get up this rock face. Go home, Riley, and tell Meabh we are all safe. I know she will be worrying her head about us.'

'Okay, lad, as long as you are alright,' he called back.

'We're fine, and the way back is quite safe. We won't have to do any climbing if we go along the valley.'

Findlaech grabbed the rope attached to the harness and they started their journey homewards. Conan ran on ahead acting as a scout and came back periodically to make sure they were keeping up.

It was a weary trio that arrived back at the feirme.

The warmth hit Findlaech as soon as he opened the door. The fire was alight, on top of the Aga was something that smelt delicious and he collapsed into the armchair exhausted but exhilarated after his evening's successful mission. It was an amazing feeling, not just to have rescued Snowy, but to have a family waiting for him at the end of the day. Again it made him realise just how lonely he had been. He smiled, leant back in the chair and savoured every last drop of stout that Riley had poured out for him.

It was days like this that made Findlaech realise just how good life could be. He couldn't believe now that he had tried to take his own life, but he knew there would be other dark days ahead.

9 One Step Too Far

Findlaech was making progress at his weekly meetings with Doctor O'Mahony. Although the medication made him feel strange at the beginning, as his body and brain adjusted to it, the dark days became less severe. Having discussed his condition in length he was starting to understand why some days he was so full of energy and enthusiasm, which was very often followed by a period of dark depression. This was the nature of Bipolar and at last he believed he could live with his condition even if there was no permanent cure.

'I think we can make the appointments once a month now, Findlaech, if you're happy with that,' O'Mahony said. 'But remember, if you feel so bad you call me straight away.'

'I will, doctor, and thank you for taking the time to talk to me.'

'You're welcome but you do need to remember however you are feeling, you cannot come off the medication, you hear me?'

'I won't, doctor, I won't.'

Findlaech stood, shook the doctor's hand, placing his cap on his unruly, straw-coloured hair before leaving the room.

Riley was waiting outside for him and his face lit up when he saw Findlaech come out smiling.

'It went well then, lad?' he asked.

'It did indeed, Riley. And he doesn't want to see me for another month.'

'That's good news indeed, well done, son.'

'You know a lot of it is down to you and Meabh, don't you Riley. I could never have got this far without you.'

Riley put his arm around Findlaech's shoulder and they walked out together like father and son.

For the first couple of months Meabh had struggled terribly with her dieting, sneaking food whenever no one was around.

'I don't understand it, Meabh, why aren't you losing weight?' Findlaech asked her one morning when she wasn't her usual perky self.

Meabh blushed and turned away in the hope that Findlaech hadn't noticed.

But of course he had noticed and he gently placed his hand on her shoulder and made her give him eye contact.

'Meabh, we made a pact, remember? You need to talk to me. After all you have listened to enough of my blubberings over the last few months.'

She did eventually lift her eyes from staring down at her hands and when she looked into Findlaech's kindly face the tears started to flow.

Just like she had done with him on one of his darkest days, he put his arms around her and gave her the biggest hug. This gentle woman had become like a second mum to him and he hated seeing her like that.

'What's wrong? Has it really been that bad? Is it living here that is getting you down?'

The questions seemed endless as they went round and round inside his head. Meabh slowly calmed and eventually found her voice so that she could answer him.

'Aw, son, this has nothing to do with you, or living here. These have been some of the best days of my life since Niamh got married.'

'Then what has upset you so much?'

'You'll think I am so weak if I tell you,' she said, her voice full of doubt.

'After everything we have been through, you must know that I would never think of you in that way. Now come on out with it or else I'll tickle it out of you.'

Findlaech had learned from Riley some time ago that Meabh hated being tickled. In fact she simply couldn't stand it and she would kick and scream if anyone was foolish enough to try.

'You just try young man, you're not too old to put over me knee you know.'

'Well come on then, spill the beans, tell me what is going on.'

She took a deep breath and sighed.

'You see, Findlaech, when you and Riley are asleep I sneak down to the kitchen and start binge eating and I just can't stop myself.'

'But there isn't really any food here that I would class as binge eating, Meabh.'

'Ah, but that's where you're wrong. When you two are out working on the feirme and you think I am just making the sourdough, I am also making scones, and biscuits, and cakes and cheese straws, all the things I love and finding impossible to live without. There, now I suppose you think I am weak.'

'Weak . . . weak . . . after what I tried to do and the way I behaved. No you are struggling just as I am and like my "depressions" your eating is also an illness and one you are going to need help with. We simply can't let your health suffer any longer.'

'Help? What sort of help can you get for overeating?'

'You'd be surprised, Meabh. Today, you can get help on virtually anything. And remember you won't have to do this on your own, Riley and meself will be with you all the way.'

Meabh wiped a stray tear from her cheek and managed a weak smile.

'Aw, son, what would I do without you.'

'Ditto,' Findlaech replied, taking her hand and giving it a squeeze. 'In the morning you'll be phoning the doc and finding out what options you have.'

Meabh simply nodded knowing he was right. She couldn't do this on her own; her willpower was not strong enough. She had watched Findlaech make such progress and this gave her hope.

It was a glorious day and for once the clouds had moved away leaving the sun to coat Sligo in its warming light. Findlaech was having a good day and whistled as he went about feeding his animals. Meabh was busy baking and Riley was sitting outside smoking his pipe with a cup of coffee in the other hand. Something had been bothering him. He knew the Ceallaigh's were good Catholic people, but he was aware they hadn't been attending church since they moved in with him. Findlaech, himself, although also once a good Catholic, had lost his faith since the death of his mother and brother. He wanted to believe in a higher being that looked after his flock, but how could he when the Almighty allowed such bad things to happen.

Once he had finished his chores, he went inside and made himself a cup of coffee and Meabh a weak green tea and asked her to come outside in the sun for a break. At first she was loath to leave her chores, but Findlaech convinced her that her bread would not ruin by having an extra ten minutes to prove. She nodded and agreed to sit with them for a while.

'Good,' said Findlaech. 'Now I have you together I want to ask you why you haven't been going to church? You are committing a sin you know.'

'You're a fine one to talk, son, I can't say you have been frequenting the place,' Riley said, puffing a plume of smoke towards the clear blue sky.'

'We're not talking about me, here. You need to keep up your faith.'

Meabh turned to look at him.

'Now don't you go and start lecturing me. I will go in my own good time, but it is important that you and Riley attend Sunday service,' Findlaech said firmly.

He smiled to himself, only a few months ago he would never have dared speak to anyone in that way. He was finding his feet and he liked it. His transformation was down to the two people sitting next to him and in an uncharacteristic gesture he took Riley's hand and then Meabh's in his other and gave them a squeeze.

'I can't begin to tell you how happy I have been since you

moved in,' he said without looking at them. 'Even on my dark days you talk me into getting out of bed and life somehow seems to look brighter.'

'Now don't you go getting all sentimental, son. You know we wouldn't have it any other way. You are the son we never had and we feel the same way,' Meabh said, squeezing his hand in return.

'Right, then, it's settled, you will go to church tomorrow and no arguing.'

'You're right, of course, we must keep up our faith, but the only way we are going to Sunday service is if you agree to come too,' Riley said firmly.

Findlaech dropped their hands, stood up and walked over to the little picket fence that led out to the paddock. He placed his hands on top of the fence, looking out to the distant mountains. How could he believe when the two people he had loved most in the world had been taken from him? How could he believe when he had been inflicted with the dreadful 'depressions'? Surely, if there were a God these things would not have happened.

He felt an arm on his shoulder and then Meabh placed her head on his shoulder.

'I know exactly what is bothering you. And you are asking why? That is the way of life, Findlaech, not necessarily God's will. After all, look what good has come out of it. We found each other and He also sent little Conan your way as a constant companion. Can't you see God is introducing you to good and bad, right and wrong, hope and despair? Give Him another chance, Findlaech. Come to Church with us tomorrow and if you still feel the same after the service we will say no more on the matter.'

Meabh was right in everything she said, but Findlaech was still struggling. He turned to his new friend, nodded and agreed to give it a go.

All bathed and done up in their Sunday best, they made a fine trio, as they climbed into the front of Riley's truck. Conan was jumping up and down and leapt in the front before anyone had a chance to restrain him.

'Not today, Conan, you need to stay here and keep an eye on the animals,' Findlaech said, grabbing hold of his collar and pulling him out of the cab. As they bounced across the rough track towards Our Lady of the Rosary Church in the Parish of Kilmactigue, Conan raced after them getting covered in a cloud of dust as the wheels purchased on the dry ground. He barked and barked, desperate not to be left out of any outing. Findlaech turned back and shook his head. Once they hit the road, they picked up speed and Conan was left standing at the end of the track with his tail between his legs.

The building itself was small, painted white with a single cross above the arched, wooden door. Inside, the pews could hold around one hundred worshippers, but on this bright, sunny Sunday, only around eight were occupied.

As they walked into the dim light, they all dipped their knees and made the sign of the cross before sitting down on the right-hand side, about halfway down the aisle. Riley and Findlaech removed their caps and placed them in their laps, dipping their heads in prayer.

Father Boyle had a sense of presence, making the

parishioners lift their heads as he walked behind the pulpit. He opened his Bible, placed his hands either side of the lectern, and leaned forward to address his flock.

'Today, dear friends, I am reading from The Baptism of the Lord and then we will discuss it's meaning.'

Father Boyle was in full flow when the congregation was disturbed by a terrible din at the front of the church. The door rattled and a loud scratching could he heard as something dragged its claws down the wood. Everyone turned round expecting the door to burst open at any moment. It was as if the Devil himself was trying to disrupt the service.

The scratching sound stopped but was followed by the sound of something being rammed up against the door and a rather incessant barking. Several times they heard the bump as something tried to break down the door. Father Boyle was making his way down the aisle when he heard the sound of the wood splintering and something bony and rounded penetrated the jagged hole.

'Goliath?' Findlay said in surprise, instantly recognising the gnarly old horn belonging to his precious ram.

The next head butt saw the door burst open and Goliath trotted in, quickly overtaken by Conan who barked loudly and jumped straight into Findlaech's lap.

Having taken his eyes off Goliath for a second, Findlaech was surprised to hear a woman scream. He looked behind him to see Goliath running back down the aisle with a mouth full of wax fruit he had extracted from the top of one of the parishioner's hats. Her husband was chasing the goat wielding his walking stick and shouting obscenities.

Meabh couldn't help herself and burst out laughing. Her laughter was infectious and soon Riley and Findlaech found it hard to keep a straight face. Conan was delighted he wasn't in trouble and licked his master's face incessantly.

Father Boyle and the lady with the partially eaten hat were not so amused.

'This is not funny. Would you please mind getting your animals under control.'

Already in a buoyant mood, Riley stood up and trying to reduce the smirk on his face, said, 'It might be a good idea to hold a service for animals once a month, then you might increase your flock.'

Father Boyle went red in the face and Meabh at once imagined steam coming out of his ears. He really was rather pompous and she was certain this wasn't what worshipping was supposed to be about.

'And I am surprised at you Riley Ceallaigh, I thought you had more decorum,' Father Boyle said, almost spitting the words out.

'Well, I've had enough of this nonsense,' Meabh said. Standing up rather too abruptly, she got her rather bulky midriff stuck between the long bench seat behind her and the one in front and could not budge.

No matter how hard Riley pushed from behind and Findlaech pulled from in front, they quite simply could not move her, not even an inch.

'That's another fine mess you've got me into,' Riley said with a grin like a Cheshire cat.

'Stop quoting Laurel and Hardy and *do* something,' Meabh

said, now embarrassed by all the attention she was receiving.

'What do you expect me to do exactly,' he replied in exasperation. He really didn't like to see his wife in this predicament.

'Have you got a screwdriver, Father Boyle?' Findlaech asked, trying to put some perspective on the situation.

Father Boyle frowned.

'I guess the answer is 'no' then?' Findlaech replied.

Riley, delving deeply into his trouser pockets, bought out an assortment of detritus, most of which was totally useless, but there was a ball of twine, a screwdriver and the ubiquitous gaffer tape, which had come in so useful before.

'Eh, voilà!' he said.

Findlaech, who had to be said was thoroughly enjoying the debacle, said 'I didn't know you could speak French?' at which comment the three of them once again burst into laughter forgetting momentarily about Meabh's predicament.

Findlaech was able to solve the problem by removing the screws from the brass plate holding the bench in place. They were then able to move one end slightly out of position; just enough for Meabh to squeeze out and hence regain her freedom.

Once unencumbered and standing in the aisle, Meabh turned to Father Boyle and said, 'Thank you Father for a most uplifting sermon. However, I have to say I do believe the highlight of this service was the arrival of Goliath and Conan. You see those animals are more loyal than any person I have ever met.'

Rather red in the face and with perspiration dripping from beneath her curly fringe, Meabh turned and waddled out of church, followed very rapidly by her husband and Findlaech.

Conan bounded ahead wagging his tail.

Once outside the three of them burst out laughing as they watched Goliath demolish Father Boyle's prize geraniums planted just outside the door.

'I haven't had such fun since our Niamh's wedding,' Riley said, holding his sides due to a painful stitch.

'I think our worship, in future, will be from the comfort of our own front room. I really can't see the need for all that pomposity and rigamarole to keep our faith,' Meabh said, linking her arms with her two favourite men.

'That's settled then, Meabh has spoken,' Riley said, bringing about another bout of laughter.

'This has been a day of healing and learning, and I do believe I can see the light!' Findlaech said with a very light heart.

10   The Elastic Band

The three of them had worked tirelessly over the autumn months, making butter, cheese, yogurt and numerous preserves made from hedgerow harvests and vegetables and fruits grown on both farms. They had more than they would need to see them through the winter so Riley suggested they took a stall at the market.

'And I've got loads of balls of wool ready to sell and numerous hats and gloves,' Meabh said, getting quite excited. 'What do you think, Findlaech?'

'You know I'm not one for showing my face in public,' he said blushing slightly at the thought.

'Nonsense, lad, you talk to us so easily, I don't think it will be a problem if we all go together.'

He didn't want to make any rash decisions, so he asked for time to think about it. He was worried it might be one of his 'down' days and he would find it hard to leave the feirme, let alone deal with strangers. It was a bit of a dilemma. He didn't want to let Riley and Meabh down, and if he were to be really honest the thought of standing behind a stall in the market terrified him.

Meabh could see the look in Findlaech's eyes and, always quick to pick up on his moods, tried to reassure him. 'I suppose you are worrying that you might have a bad day.'

How did she do that, he thought. It's spooky she always seems to know what I am thinking. He looked at her and nodded.

'Why don't we make a deal then. If you wake up and you know the day is going to be difficult, then Riley and meself will go and sell the goods. However, if you wake up and it is one of your positive days, I would like you to try and face your demons. After all, look how well you did that day in church. You weren't fazed at all.'

She was right, of course, he hadn't thought twice about going into the church and facing those people. When he felt upbeat, he knew he could face most situations if he had Meabh and Riley by his side.

'It's a deal,' he said, presenting her the palm of his hand in a high five.

'If you haven't got any jobs outside to do, I don't suppose you could help me bottle up this tomato chutney? I find the preserving pan a little too heavy to hold.'

They worked together for the next hour, bottling up hot preserves, placing small circles of greaseproof paper on the top, finally sealing the lid tightly. Meabh had made pretty lid coverings by cutting circles of fabric and finishing off the edges with a pair of pinking shears.

'They look grand, Meabh,' Riley said, coming into the warm kitchen.

'Boots, Mr Ceallaigh,' Meabh barked as soon as he had stepped foot inside the door.

He had too much respect to answer back and dutifully turned round, removed his boots and placed them in the small porch. Conan followed him in and stopped to sniff the inside of the boots. He turned his nose up and walked away, causing the three of them to burst out laughing.

'You know what?' Riley said.

'No, what?' Meabh asked.

'We are getting really good at laughing recently.'

'Well, they say laughter is the best medicine, and I truly believe the old saying is right,' Findlaech said. 'As each week goes by my moods are getting less severe. If I do have a bad day, with your help I seem to be able to shrug them off instead of sinking into the depths of despair.'

'That's great news,' said Meabh. 'And I have a bit of news meself. I have an appointment with a consultant on Monday, the doc phoned me this morning.'

'That is good news. That means you will soon be getting help as well,' Findlaech said.

Next week they had a couple of appointments; Monday was a trip to the hospital and Saturday was a morning at the market.

Meabh and Riley sat nervously outside the consultant's room. Neither of them had any idea what he would suggest, but they would welcome any help they could get if it would improve her health.

She tried reading one of the magazines on farming, but she couldn't concentrate and her eyes kept going to the plaque on the consultant's door – DR FREDERICK POLLARD, CONSULTANT GENERAL SURGEON. The words 'General Surgeon' unnerved her a little. What kind of surgery were they talking about that could help her with her overeating? It was going round and round in her head when the door opened and a tiny man with a rather squeaky voice called out her name.

Meabh stood up and had to tap Riley on the shoulder to get his attention. He had been watching a television screen giving the local news and hadn't heard his wife's name being called. He immediately stood, took his wife's arm and led her into the consulting room.

'Good morning Mr and Mrs Ceallaigh, please take a seat,' indicating two chairs in front of his large wooden desk.

On one corner of the desk was an old computer, on which the consultant was tapping out some letters on the keyboard. His half glasses were perched on the end of his nose, and he looked over the top as he stared at the screen.

'Now Mrs Ceallaigh, I understand from your doctor you would like some help with your diet. Before we start would you mind standing on the scales over there?'

Meabh took off her shoes in the hope that it would make a difference to her weight, even though she knew it was a futile exercise.

She waddled over to the scales, lifted one swollen leg onto the plate and heaved the other one up with difficulty onto the small platform. When she saw the needle swing violently to the right she almost burst into tears.

Dr Pollard walked over, checked the dial and returned to his desk without saying a word. Again he punched some statistics into his computer.

'Thank you, Mrs Ceallaigh, perhaps you would like to sit down again.'

There was a pause before he said anything again and Meabh felt as if he were judging her and made her feel uncomfortable. She almost grabbed her bag and rushed out of the doctor's office, but Riley must have sensed how she was feeling and he put a comforting hand on her arm.

'Right, Mrs Ceallaigh . . . may I call you Meabh?'

'Please do Doctor Pollard, it might make it feel less formal,' Riley said, speaking up for his wife.

The consultant also seemed to pick up on his patient's discomfort and his demeanour immediately changed. He relaxed his shoulders, trying to forget his demanding schedule, and remembering the lesson he had been taught that each patient is an individual and hence needs to be treated that way. He immediately stopped looking at his computer screen, removed his glasses, and placed his hands comfortably on top of the desk.

'Now, Meabh, please don't feel alarmed. I would like to help you lose some of that weight so that it puts less of a strain on your heart and your legs.'

'She does need help, doctor,' Riley stressed. 'She finds it so hard to control her cravings, you see.'

Doctor Pollard nodded and smiled.

'I think the best way to treat the problem is by doing bariatric surgery, Meabh, but that in itself does not come without its problems. I am going to give you a leaflet to read so that you can understand the trade-off between the outcome and the risks involved.'

'Surgery!' Riley said in alarm.

'Please don't worry, it is perfectly safe and will control the urge to eat too much. In fact you won't be able to eat too much because your stomach will be so much smaller,' the consultant tried to explain, seeing the look of abject horror on his patient's face. He knew he needed to try and soften the blow; he could see this particular patient was struggling.

'I . . . I . . . I'm not sure I like the sound of that.' Again it was Riley who expressed his opinion as Meabh was in a state of shock at the mention of surgery. She shouldn't have been, otherwise why would she have been sent to see a consultant surgeon.

'Let me try to explain more about the procedure we use. The operation involves me putting an adjustable band around the top part of your stomach. Because it creates a small pouch at the top of the stomach, when you eat it is only this part that will fill up with food instead of the complete stomach. This means you will feel full a lot quicker taking away your desire to keep eating. That feeling of being full will also last a lot longer so that you will find it easier to stick to three regular meals a day instead of snacking in between. Mind you, it will depend on your determination as well. You will need to change your lifestyle and certainly your eating habits. However, this will get easier each day as the hunger subsides to a normal level. Once you have lost a couple of stone you will find it so much easier to increase your exercise without risking your legs becoming ulcerated.' He paused to allow this information to sink in. 'Of course it would be wrong of me not to explain the disadvantages, but I do believe in your case it would be most beneficial.'

Meabh was quiet and pale as she listened to Doctor Pollard explaining the possible side effects. However, the more she thought about it, the more it made sense to try and shrink her stomach to control her cravings. She knew she could not continue as she was and she certainly wasn't ready to meet her maker just yet.

'The surgery is done by keyhole surgery, which means we won't be opening you up and you can go home the same day once we are happy you are over the anaesthetic. You won't feel anything other than a slight discomfort which we can alleviate with the help of analgesics. Do you have any questions, Meabh?'

'Will I have to come and see you after the operation?' she asked nervously.

'Yes, you will need regular appointments to make sure everything is going to plan. As you lose weight I will inject fluids into the gastric band to further reduce your stomach, until we have your eating under control. How does that sound to you Meabh?'

'It's a lot to take in, but I am happy you are suggesting what is right for me,' she said, thinking about Findlaech and all he had been through.

'That's good, Meabh, and I am so glad you have agreed to give it a go. I have a slot next Wednesday if you are happy to come in. We will carry out some routine tests and if all is well we will perform the procedure early in the morning so you are ready to go home by the evening.'

Riley took her hand, patted it gently, trying to give her the encouragement she so desperately needed.

They both thanked the doctor and said they would arrive at Outpatients the following Wednesday. The consultant gave Meabh a leaflet answering any questions she might have, but he said to ring him if there was anything she was uncertain of.

The drive home to Aclare was quiet, as they both mulled over what they had been told in the consulting room.

'It'll be alright, you see,' Riley said, trying to convince himself as well as his wife.

When they arrived home, Findlaech had made a fresh fruit salad as a treat and was in the process of brewing a pot of tea.

'Well, how did it go?' he asked impatiently.

'Aw, lad, I've got to have an elastic band fitted.'

She saw the look of complete confusion on Findlaech's face.

Riley tried not to laugh. 'Not an *elastic* band, girl, a *gastric* band!'

Still none the wiser, Findlaech started to laugh, immediately seeing the funny side. It wasn't long before all three were belly laughing about her *faux pas*, helping put the stress of the day behind them.

'Let me read the leaflet, Meabh, and that way perhaps I can understand this procedure a little better,' Findlaech said.

If he were to be honest he didn't like the sound of it but he wasn't going to let on to his two friends. He needed to remain positive for them, just as they had for him. So with more enthusiasm than he actually felt, he said, 'You're going to be fine Meabh, not everyone gets a chance to get a new body. You'll have all the boys whistling after you soon.'

'Aw, get away with you boy, you've lost your senses,' she said, but still found it hard to keep a straight face.

Their laughter could be heard all over the yard and the animals all pricked up their ears. It was not a sound they were used to hearing before the arrival of Meabh and Riley.

11 A Pair of Pale Blue Eyes

Market day arrived and Riley's truck was loaded up to the gunnels. The market provided the table and an awning, which was a good thing as there wasn't an inch to spare in the back. The front was pretty cramped, too, once the three of them had climbed into the cabin, not helped by a rather insistent Conan who was not going to be left behind under any circumstances.

They bumped up the track over the rough stone surface. The jars rattled in their crates and Meabh was concerned they would break before they even reached the market.

'You're worrying over nothing, Ma,' Riley said trying to calm her down, 'I packed them carefully and there is plenty of newspaper in between each jar.'

Meabh dropped her shoulders, rolled them backwards and took a deep breath. Riley knew it wasn't the jars she was concerned about; she would be getting herself in a state about the operation on Wednesday to have the 'elastic' band fitted, as she called it. As if aware of her state of hypertension, Conan pushed past Findlaech and started to lick her cheek.

'Aw, be away with you, Conan, I don't need another wash,' Meabh said pushing him away gently.

The rest of the journey was fairly uneventful except for Conan's rather bad bout of flatulence, causing both Findlaech and Riley to open their windows rather promptly to make a through draught.

'Oh pooh, Conan, that's disgusting!' Meabh exclaimed

holding her nose. 'That's the last time I let you lick the curry pot clean. Now poke your backside out the window if you are going to do that again.'

They all laughed and once again discovered just how good they were at lifting one another's spirits. Findlaech had started the day well and, although a little anxious regarding facing people at the market, he knew with his two new friends backing him he would get through the day.

The market at Kilkelly was bustling with everyone busy setting up their stalls. Wonderful smells wafted in the air as the food stalls started preparing for the breakfast rush. Meabh sniffed the air as she laid out her jars of preserve, squares of honeycomb, sweet and savoury scones, cakes, pasties, sausage rolls, cheese, yogurt and any food related items on one table, while to her right Riley and Findlaech displayed all her other works of art from knitting to embroidery and even a beautiful tapestry which Findlaech had framed for her using a piece of carved oak. Riley pinned some red and green fairy lights around the front of the stall and then started putting the small cardboard price tags in front of each item. By the time they had finished it looked really professional and they settled back into the canvas chairs they had bought with them.

Riley went off to get some coffees and came back with a cardboard try laden with goodies.

'Before you say anything, I am not encouraging Meabh to eat bad things, but today is a good day and I want to spoil her. Soon she will have to be very careful about what she eats,' Riley said before either of them made a comment.

Findlaech held his hands up in submission. 'I totally agree, today we will spoil ourselves and, as from Wednesday, we will all be on a healthy diet to encourage Meabh to lose weight.'

'Cheers,' Meabh said holding her cardboard cup aloft.

There was silence as the three of them tucked into bacon, egg and black pudding baguettes. The bread was so fresh and crusty and Meabh savoured every mouthful, occasionally wiping the rich yellow egg yolk from her chin.

'Ooh Da, that was simply the best,' she said.

'Mmmmm, it really was,' Findlaech agreed. It was so rare for him to eat anything that wasn't healthy; he too relished each bite.

The market was filling up and every table and chair held someone savouring all the breakfast goodies on offer. Once service was over, the stalls starting preparing for the busy lunch trade and with full bellies people started to wander around the stalls, pausing at each one to see what was on offer.

It was soon so busy Findlaech, Meabh and Riley all had to serve customers. Findlaech soon forgot his nerves as he started to explain how they made their cheese and yogurt. In fact he found it all quite exhilarating and was quickly in his stride.

Patrick Quinn, a good friend of Riley's and manning the stall next to theirs, was shocked to see the change in Findlaech. He hadn't seen him since Byrne's funeral, when he had spoken to no one and simply stood in the corner not giving anyone eye contact. What had changed the young man? He intended to ask Riley later.

Accompanying Patrick on their stall was his wife Shauna and their daughter Clodagh. When Shauna was pregnant during her last semester the baby became stressed and the doctor had to perform a caesarean section before the end of term. Baby Clodagh was tiny, weighing only 4 lb 4 oz and had to go straight into an incubator. It was a worrying time for the family who had tried for so long to have a baby. On the third day, Shauna was sitting by the incubator waiting to give her baby a feed when she noticed her skin had gone a strange tinge of blue and then she started to convulse. She screamed for a nurse, who immediately called the paediatrician who administered a drug into her tiny veins and put an oxygen mask over her face.

'What's happening Shauna asked,' afraid to hear the answer.

'I'm afraid your baby has had a seizure. It can happen with premature babies, but we seem to have it under control now.'

Against all odds Clodagh survived another seizure and had to stay in intensive care for the first year of her life. It left her weak and very vulnerable to infection and had to take medication to keep the seizures under control. Her left arm didn't work well and her brain was minimally damaged, which meant she struggled with her schoolwork. She left at sixteen, not wanting to cope with any exams and now worked hard helping her mother and father on the farm, producing delicious sausages, bacon and numerous joints of pork which they sold in their local farm shop and at the various markets.

Riley and Meabh knew the Quinn family well and had always treated Clodagh as one of their own. Patrick used to drop her off to play with their daughter, Niamh, and they would spend hours in her room making up imaginary games with dolls and teddies. The two of them were like sisters, Clodagh drawing strength from her friend. The pair became inseparable and Meabh was aware it was quite a wrench when their daughter got married. Clodagh had to adjust to being on her own again.

As the market began to quieten down for lunch, Meabh went to speak with the Quinns.

'Hello Meabh,' Shauna said, giving her friend a big hug.

'Sorry we haven't been such good friends of late, Shauna, but you see we moved in with Findlaech to give him a hand.'

'And looking at him, it has done him the world of good,' Patrick replied. 'I have never seen the young man so confident and look, he's laughing. It's a miracle.'

'Yes, he is making progress with his 'depressions' with the help of a doctor at the hospital,' Meabh told them proudly. She decided to say nothing about her own health problems and hopefully the next time she saw them she too would be making some progress.

Clodagh, who was exceptionally shy, was sitting at the back of the stall eating an ice cream. Meabh waved and asked if she was all right. Clodagh nodded and went back to reading her magazine.

Meabh called Findlaech over to say hello to the Quinns. Any other day he would probably have gone red but today had been a good day and he had learned how to speak with other people without feeling awkward. He took the bull by the horns, came out from behind his table and shook Patrick and Shauna's hands politely. He didn't remember ever meeting their daughter, but when she looked up from her magazine and smiled at him, the pale blue eyes that met his took his breath away.

'Findlaech, I don't believe you know Clodagh,' Meabh said.

Findlaech so wanted to say something to her, but that look had unbalanced him and he couldn't find the right words. She was the prettiest young woman he had ever seen, with her auburn curls and rosebud cheeks. Meabh, aware of the change in Findlaech, nudged him in the ribs in the hope she could get his attention.

'Shauna was asking how you are getting on,' Meabh said at last getting him to turn away from Clodagh.

'Aw fine, Mrs Quinn, just fine. With the help of my two friends here, life is looking up.' He gave her the biggest smile because in his heart he meant every word.

Later that day when they were packing up the stall, Findlaech noticed Clodagh walking past to put some rubbish in one of the communal bins. As she passed she dropped a cardboard box and Findlaech was out from behind his table in a flash. He picked up the box which Clodagh was unaware she had dropped, and ran to catch up with her.

'Clodagh! Clodagh!' he called after her.

At first she didn't respond, but as it registered someone was calling her name she stopped and turned around.

'You . . . you . . . dropped this,' he said a little nervously.

'Thank you, Findlaech,' she said very politely.

Findlaech thought her voice just as beautiful as her face, the words drifting off into the breeze. He had never really thought very much about women, he always imagined he would live on his own, but for some reason this beautiful Irish lass was getting his heart all a flutter.

'Here, let me help you,' Findlaech said, taking some of the

boxes from the top. He walked with Clodagh to the bins and not wanting her to leave tried to start up a conversation. 'Have you finished packing up your stall?'

He could see she wasn't finding it easy and he watched as the sweetest flush turned her cheeks a pretty shade of pink.

Without giving him any eye contact she nodded her head.

'Would you like a glass of lemonade?' he asked hopefully.

Again she nodded and Findlaech's heart leapt a little in his chest.

'That's great Clodagh, but first I think we should tell your Ma and Pa where we are going.'

Again this was greeted with just a nod, but Findlaech was not put off, in fact he found it most endearing. If she had been streetwise and a flirt he knew he would not have been at all interested. It was the fact that she was so naive and innocent that he found Clodagh so intriguing.

They walked back to the stall and Findlaech politely went to ask Patrick if he could take Clodagh over to the lemonade stall for some refreshment. Patrick's face lit up, no one had ever really taken any interest in Clodagh she was always the wilting wallflower sitting in the background.

'That would be great, Findlaech. You will find us over by the dark red truck when you are ready.'

When they reached the lemonade stall, Findlaech asked Clodagh if she would like to sit on one of the white plastic chairs while he went to get the drinks. Still not looking up from her feet she nodded and went to sit down. He had to think how he felt only a few months ago and was determined to try and encourage her out of herself.

Once he was seated opposite her, he decided asking too many questions was probably not a good idea at the moment. Conan, who had followed him, was sitting next Clodagh and to Findlaech's delight he saw she was stroking the top of his head.

'His name's Conan.'

He thought he saw a smile starting to form on her lips, but still he couldn't get a response.

'Shall I tell you a funny story about him?'

Clodagh nodded.

Findlaech went on to tell her about the time he had chased Goliath his big goat and how he had been tossed into the air. He also told her about how he had saved his life by going to get help, leaving out the bit that he had tried to take his own life. 'You see he is a very special dog, if a little wayward at times.'

Little by little, the more he talked, he noticed Clodagh starting to relax. She looked up from stroking Conan to take a sip of her lemonade through the yellow striped straw.

'Do you have any pets?' Findlaech asked.

'Only the pigs, but they're not really pets,' she said, still unable to make eye contact.

'No, I suppose they're not. But I think of all my animals as pets so I can understand what you are saying.'

'Tell me some more stories,' she said. 'I like your stories.'

And that was the way they spent the next half hour – Findlaech talking and Clodagh listening. In fact they were so engrossed they didn't notice Clodagh's father until he put his hand on Findlaech's shoulder.

'I am sorry to break this up, but I am afraid we have to leave now Clodagh. Mother wants to get home so she can get dinner ready and I have to go and feed the pigs.'

Clodagh stood dutifully and went to stand beside her father. Findlaech thought she was going to walk away without saying anything, but she surprised him by actually giving him eye contact and saying, 'I do hope I see you again soon, Findlaech. Thank you so much for the lemonade.'

In fact Findlaech was so taken aback by this unexpected response for a couple of seconds he was lost for words. He nearly had to pinch himself that it had actually happened. Up until a few months ago nice things didn't happen to him.

'Clodagh, I would love to see you soon. Perhaps your father would permit me to take you to the cinema in town. I will find out which films are showing.'

You could have knocked Patrick over with a feather. Not only was this so out of character for his daughter, but he had never in all his years seen Findlaech say more than two words. This time it was Patrick who was lost for words.

'Young man, it would be just dandy for you to take our Clodagh to the films. What do you say Clodagh?' He didn't want to be presumptuous and just assume his daughter would like to go. But as soon as he saw her face light up with a beautiful smile he already had his answer.

'Perfect. I will find out what film is showing and if you are happy with my choice, Clodagh, I will arrange a time and date.'

She repeated his word, 'Perfect.'

By the time Findlaech got back to the stall everything had been cleared away. In actual fact there wasn't much to clear away as they had sold virtually everything.

He felt as light as a feather and his heart sang with joy.

'Oh Meahb, this has been such a good day,' and he gave her the biggest hug.

'Indeed it has,' she said linking her arm through his and together they walked back to the truck singing a little tune – *Always Look on the Bright Side of Life.*

'What's got you two in such a good mood?' Riley asked, watching them almost skipping across the grass towards him.

'Oh I don't know, Riley, maybe its just life. Maybe after all these years I have learnt to live. I could never have done it without you two you know and, if you will allow it of course, I would like to call you Ma and Da.'

The tears that sprung from Meabh's eyes would have burst a dam and even Riley was having a hard job holding it together.

'Aw son, you really are the boy we never had and for that we will always be thankful. Today really is one of the best.'

12 A Weight Off My Mind

Wednesday was a day of mixed emotions. Meabh was anxious about the operation but also couldn't wait to see what difference it made. She knew if only she could lose a few stone in weight she would feel so much better. At the moment her legs were sore with ulcers and she struggled every day to try and do the most menial of tasks. It was decided just Riley would take her to hospital so Findlaech could get on with his chores, but they were both coming to pick her up and there was to be no arguing on that matter.

'Come here, son, and give me a hug before I leave. That way I can remember it when they put me under.'

'You'll be fine, Ma, you'll be fine,' Findlaech said, trying to convince himself more than Meabh.

'Of course I will. I'm as strong as an ox you know.'

Riley stayed with her until they took her down to the operating theatre then he sat in the waiting room anxious to learn how the procedure had gone. There was no way he was going home until he knew that his precious wife was all right. He tried to sit, but he had restless legs and paced up and down quite a lot, drinking numerous cups of disgustingly weak coffee from the vending machine in the corner.

It seemed hours later when a nurse came to find him.

'Your wife is out of theatre now Mr Ceallaigh and everything went well. She will need some rest so we suggest you go home and we will call you when she is ready to see you. She will be a bit sore for a while but we will make sure she is comfortable.'

Riley hadn't realised he had been wringing his cap in his hands and his mouth had the metallic taste of blood where he had bitten his bottom lip. He gradually let himself relax and thanked the nurse. He drove home feeling a lot happier than when they had arrived that morning.

Findlaech was delighted to hear that everything had gone well and he made a couple of omelettes and steaming mugs of hot chocolate to welcome him home. They sat and talked about what to do for the rest of the day. They had a log store to build, some fences to mend and Riley wanted to go and pick up some young chickens to add to their little flock. However, all this went out of the window when Conan came running into the kitchen, spinning in circles and pulling on the bottom of Findlaech's trousers. They knew only too well by now that this meant something was amiss, so they both stood up and followed him outside.

Conan pushed the small gate open that led into the paddock and ran through the long grass full of wild flowers, leaving streaks of yellow pollen across his back and sides. Riley and Findlaech followed as fast as they could. The dog led them down to the river where Goliath and Snowy had come for a drink. They shouldn't have been able to reach the river but a bad storm had damaged one section of the fencing enclosing the paddock and Goliath had his leg tangled up in some wire. The more he pulled, the tighter the wire became entangled in his fur until it started to cut into his skin.

'You hold him still if you can while I go and get a pair of pliers. We need to get him out of this mess before he really hurts himself,' Riley said, walking as quickly as his ageing legs would allow.

Findlaech climbed down the bank until he was level with Goliath and tried with all his might to keep him still. That was easier said than done as the enormous goat bellowed and tried to butt him with his enormous curved horns. He talked to him in a soothing manner, attempting to calm the animal down, but he wasn't having much effect and he knew any minute he was going to end up in the water.

He was just about to give up and wait for Riley to get back when, once again, Conan saved the day. He had picked up on the goat's agitation and instead of barking and going mad, he jumped onto Goliath's back and started to knead him with his paws. It was the most unusual thing Findlaech had ever seen, but somehow it worked. The sensation on the goat's back seemed to calm him down and he became still, his eyes almost closed, almost as if in a trance.

'Whatever you are doing, Conan, keep doing it. Good boy.'

Findlaech sat back on the damp earth of the riverbank and watched in fascination. 'I think I will call you the 'goat whisperer' Conan, you certainly seem to have the touch. Wherever did you learn that?'

Riley was back in no time with some pliers and a pair of wire cutters.

He was about to shoo Conan off when he too realised what was happening. He stood stock still not quite sure whether his eyes were playing tricks with him.

'Well I never, I have never seen anything like it in me life.'

'He saved the day again, Pa, I couldn't hold Goliath any

longer and Conan just jumped on his back and somehow got him to calm down.'

'Amazing. That dog will never cease to amaze me. He might do some crazy things sometimes, but then he goes and makes up for it by acting like this.'

'Stay there, Conan, while we try and get this wire off his leg,' Findlaech said, patting his dog on the back.

Together using the pliers and wire cutters they managed to cut the wire and work it loose. It had made a nasty cut in his skin, which had turned the white fur red in places, but they knew that would heal with a little antiseptic. It could have been so much worse.

Findlaech tied a rope around the goat's neck and led him slowly back to the yard so they could bathe the wound and administer some antiseptic ointment to stop the cut from festering. As soon as they were happy the wound was clean, they bandaged the leg and placed Goliath and Snowy in the barn for the night so he wouldn't get into any further trouble.

As for Conan, he got the biggest bone Findlaech could find out of the cupboard and left him chewing it happily outside the back door.

Before they had to return to the hospital the two men managed to repair the broken fence and have a well-earned cup of tea. They washed and changed and headed off to pick up their precious Meabh.

On arriving home they settled Ma onto the temporary bed they had made for her in the living room. They made her put her feet up and placed big plump pillows behind her back and neck. She was much quieter than normal, which was only to be expected, and was more than happy for her two men to spoil her. She was in a little bit of discomfort but she had medication to control the pain and the surgeon had told her she could get back to her normal life in about six weeks.

The nurse had given Meabh a booklet to explain what to expect after surgery and for the first two to three weeks she could only eat liquid or puréed food so that her stomach didn't reject it.

'Right, and no arguing, I am going to be in charge of your diet until you are ready to take over cooking duties again,' Findlaech said, determined to help her through this difficult time.

'There'll be no argument from me,' Meabh said.

'Nor me,' Riley confirmed. 'Only too happy to let you take over. I will be here to play games, read to you, or whatever takes your fancy my love.'

Meabh managed a weak smile but said she really needed to sleep if that was OK. So they decided to go and feed the animals and bed them down for the night while she got some rest.

That evening they all watched a film and then, making sure Meabh was comfortable before they went upstairs, retired for the night.

The next six weeks were a bit of a challenge but they all remained positive and once Meabh was up and about and able to eat normal meals, albeit a fraction of what she used to eat, she started to feel really positive. Her skirts started to feel loser around her middle, her blouses didn't bulge over her bosom and week by week they all noticed a difference.

Every day they all went for a walk and Meabh said once she had lost some more weight she would like to start riding the bike. Riley changed the dressings on her legs and was amazed to see the ulcers had already started to heal over. He added new dressings using natural honey and told her that in another couple of weeks he felt she wouldn't need to wear bandages any more.

One morning Findlaech was up extremely early before anyone else was awake. He grabbed a quick sandwich, made himself a flask of coffee. He left a note on the kitchen table to say he had gone on an errand and wouldn't be back until late afternoon so not to worry. It was times like this that he wished he could drive instead of having to rely on his bike, but it was a beautiful day and the exercise would do him good. He set off in good spirits and, once off the rough track that led to the feirme the surface was smoother and he made good progress. His aim was to reach the coast where he knew the trawlers would be bringing in their catches. He wanted to buy the biggest lobster as a special treat for Meabh now she was able to eat normal food. It took him almost two hours to reach the coast and he watched as the fishing boats anchored and the fishermen waded ashore with the day's catch. Findlaech's efforts were rewarded with two whopping lobsters which he placed in the panniers on either side of the cross bar.

Riding home was harder because a lot of it was uphill, but even when he felt like giving up he pumped his legs to bring his treasures home. Meabh had been a trooper and never complained even on the days when she must have felt rough, and this was the least he could do.

'Where do you think he has gone?' Meabh asked. 'He didn't say anything about any errands to me.'

'He doesn't have to tell us everything you know,' Riley said in his defence. 'Maybe it has something to do with Clodagh. I do believe he is quite taken by that young lass.'

They both turned when Conan started jumping up and down and barking. He flew out of the kitchen as if his tail was on fire and ran down the lane away from the feirme.

'That must be Findlaech then,' Riley said.

Conan had been sitting waiting patiently by the back door not moving until he could sense his master was home.

He came bounding in a few minutes later followed by a very red-faced Findlaech.

'What have you been up to, Findlaech, your face is very red?' Meabh asked.

'It's those damn hills. It's hard going when your bicycle only has three gears,' he replied.

'It's about time I taught you to drive, Findlaech. We will start in the morning. We can just drive round the farm and up the track until you get your licence,' Riley said, realising he should have suggested it sooner.

'Really! Fantastic.'

'Now, tell me where you have been, I'm busting to know,' Meabh asked.

Findlaech held up the two bulging panniers and grinned. 'I've bought you a present.'

Meabh couldn't contain her excitement and peered into the panniers. 'Lobster! I absolutely adore lobster. Don't tell me you cycled all the way to the coast, son.'

'Yes, and it is worth every aching muscle just to see your face.'

'My mouth is watering already,' and she rushed and gave Findlaech the hugest hug. He had got used to these shows of affection and they no longer seemed unnatural to him.

'And, no arguing, I am cooking tonight. Salad and lobster and a nice bottle of sparkling wine. We are celebrating your health.'

They all laughed and cheered. It had indeed been worth the effort. These were the best times, not just for Findlaech, but for Meabh and Riley too who were happier than they had been in a long while.

After six months the transformation was evident. Meabh no longer wanted to eat big portions or indeed snack between meals because she just wasn't hungry. She had joined a local keep fit class in the village hall and a couple of people had walked past her in the street, not recognising the new Meabh. She had never been happier. As for Riley he felt he had a new wife. Because they had all been eating sensibly, Riley had lost some weight too and he felt like a young man again, ready to take on the world.

Although Findlaech struggled some days with his 'depressions', instead of hiding himself away, he talked it through with Ma and Pa, and gradually his mood lifted enough so he could get through the day.

He had discussed in length whether or not he should take Clodagh out because he didn't want to scare her off with his moods, but they had both reassured him that she had problems too and they were certain it would be a good thing. Having explained to Patrick that he needed to be around while Meabh was recovering, he wasn't sure whether Clodagh would still be interested in going to the cinema.

A few weeks after Meabh's operation, Findlaech cycled to the Quinns to tell Clodagh that the Curzon was showing a rerun of *The Best Exotic Marigold Hotel*, and to ask her whether she would like to go. Shauna answered the door and invited Findlaech inside while she went to fetch her daughter.

'Hello, Findlaech,' Clodagh said, not looking at her feet this time but able to give him eye contact.

'Hello, Clodagh. I have called round to see if you would like to go and see a film tomorrow evening? Sorry it has taken so long.'

'I would love that,' she said smiling.

'I am afraid I don't drive but Riley said he would drop us off at seven thirty if that is all right with you. We will come and pick you up at seven.'

'Lovely,' she said.

Findlaech didn't know what else to say, he had never dated a girl before. 'OK then, I will see you tomorrow, at seven.'

He cycled home excited, but also extremely nervous and wasn't certain he had done the right thing. She was definitely very pretty, and she certainly gave him butterflies in his stomach, but it was all so alien to him and he wasn't sure how to handle it.

Once again he turned to his Ma and Pa to get advice. After all they had dated when they first met and perhaps they could give him some useful tips.

'Aw, Findlaech, it was so long ago Ma and me had a date I don't know what advice to give you,' Riley said. 'If I remember rightly it just seemed to come natural with Meabh; you know as if I had known her a long time.'

'Findlaech, just be yourself. Take it slowly, get to know her properly and if it is meant to be it will be,' Meabh said adding her bit of wisdom.

'You are right, I will try to relax and just be myself. I just hope that myself is good enough though.'

'Good enough!' Riley exclaimed. 'You are a fine young man with impeccable manners and any young lass would be lucky to have you.'

'Now don't go overdoing it, Da, remember me 'depressions'. I am not so sure Clodagh would be lucky but if I can make her laugh I will be happy.'

Riley dropped them at the Curzon and told them he would be back at ten o'clock, giving them time to go and get something to eat after the film.

Clodagh was very quiet at first and once again was finding it hard to look directly at Findlaech. Hopefully she would relax once they were inside and it was dark. He knew how hard she must be finding it, after all neither of them had been on a date before and he was struggling.

As they sat down the sweetest scent of rosewater reached Findlaech's nostrils and he so wanted to run his fingers through her beautiful curls. He had bought a large tub of popcorn which he balanced on his lap and told Clodagh to just dive in when she fancied some.

They sat in silence and watched the opening advertisements and then as the main film started he was aware of Clodagh resting her head on the back of the seat. He hoped that meant she was starting to relax. She eventually plucked up enough courage to have some of the popcorn and soon they had eaten the whole tub between them. Findlaech was finding it hard to actually concentrate on the film, he was so aware of Clodagh next to him and the heat of her thigh as it touched his. He thought she would move her leg away, but he was so pleased to know she was comfortable enough to leave it where it was.

He could see she was engrossed in the film and occasionally he looked her way to make sure she was happy.

Shortly before the film ended, Findlaech was brave enough to reach for her hand. He was unsure what reaction he would get and was pleasantly surprised when she allowed him to take it in his. He squeezed her fingers gently and she turned and gave him the most beautiful smile. Findlaech was in heaven.

After the film they went to a tiny burger restaurant a few doors down. Clodagh took a seat while Findlaech ordered. He took a seat opposite so that he could see her beautiful pale blue eyes.

'Did you enjoy the film, Clodagh?' he asked.

'Oh yes, Findlaech, I did enjoy it so much. What about you?'

He didn't want to say she had been too much of a distraction for him to concentrate, so he just answered, 'Perfect.'

After they had finished eating and Findlaech had told her a few more funny stories about his farm he took her hand across the table. 'I have really enjoyed tonight, Clodagh, would you let me take you out again?'

He thought she had blushed a little, but that was part of her appeal. She nodded, 'I would love that Findlaech.'

They stood hand in hand waiting for Riley to pick them up and wanting to show her he had manners, when they arrived at her house, Findlaech jumped out of the truck, opened the door and took her hand while she climbed down.

'I would like to go dancing,' she said looking him directly in the face. 'You see I have only been dancing once and that was with Ma and Da.'

Findlaech's heart dropped a little. He had never danced, didn't even know how to dance, and Clodagh picked up on his mood.

'Don't you want to go, Findlaech?'

'Oh, yes, I want to go very much, but you see I have never been dancing and I don't think I would be very good at it,' determined to be truthful about how he felt. The only way he knew was to be honest about everything.

'I will teach you, don't be scared.'

Findlaech smiled.

'Be patient with me then if I tread on your toes.'

Clodagh took his hand and then leant forward and placed the gentlest kiss on his cheek. It was as if a butterfly had brushed its wings against his skin. It was probably the most beautiful kiss he had ever had. He wanted to take her in his arms and hold her, but he held back not wanting to spoil the moment.

13 The Relapse

Since his date with Clodagh, Findlaech had been on cloud nine. He only had two more days to go before he was taking her to the dance and he was counting down the hours. He was nervous, after all he had never been dancing, but with Meabh's help he had learnt the basics and could now hold her comfortably as he swung her round to the music.

Needless to say this had been a huge source of laughter to them, especially when Conan decided to join in. He barked and barked and jumped up on his hind legs, convinced that he was human and able to dance.

'Will you look at that dog,' Riley said as he watched his wife and Findlaech cavorting round the living room. He was amazed how slim Meabh was now, in fact she had lost so much weight they decided to go into town and buy her some new clothes. She was ecstatic when she held up her old elasticated skirt to show just how much weight she had lost.

'If you are going into town then I'm coming with you,' Findlaech said. 'I definitely need a new outfit for the dance.'

'Then that's decided, tomorrow morning we will head off to town and help one another choose an outfit,' Meabh said.

The surgeon was so pleased with her progress he told her he didn't want to see her for another six months and that she should continue exactly as she had been.

'You know what, I'm going to spoil meself with a nice steaming cup of hot chocolate,' Meabh said after her appointment. 'The doc said I only have two more stone to lose and then I will be at my optimum weight. This is a day to celebrate. A day to celebrate indeed.'

They all sat at the kitchen table and discussed what they were going to buy for themselves, using some of the proceeds they had made at the market.

'I want some black trousers and a shirt and, if there is enough money left over, perhaps a pair of smart shoes. You know I haven't bought anything new since Ma died all those years ago.'

'You spoil yourself, Findlaech, you deserve it son,' Riley said sipping his chocolate.

Thursday morning arrived, the day they were all going shopping. Riley was up early and fed all the animals, let them out into the paddock and then came indoors to have breakfast.

'No Findlaech?' Riley asked, a frown creasing his forehead.

'No, it is unusual. Do you think I should go up and check he is all right?'

'Leave it to me. I wanted to tell him he could drive into town now he has his licence.'

'Oh he will be so excited,' Meabh said.

Riley climbed the stairs with trepidation. Findlaech had been having several good weeks but, because Conan hadn't come downstairs either, he was certain this was going to be one of his bad days. He wasn't sure how to approach him, to make him feel better, and he wished he had allowed Meabh to come instead. She always handled situations like this so much better than he did.

Even though the sun was up and the dawn chorus produced a cheery tune outside his window, inside his head the day was black. Nothing was going to penetrate the dark blanket that had descended over his brain this morning and he didn't even bother to try and lift his head from the pillow. When he had gone to sleep last night the morning had seemed so full of promise. Spending the day with his two best friends choosing new clothes for his date. He was also excited about seeing Meabh in some new blouses and skirts; it lifted his heart to see her so well.

However, these thoughts were not in his mind when he woke up in the early hours of the morning. He wasn't sure what had woken him, whether it was the blinding headache, or the dark, dark thoughts that told him he was a useless individual and shouldn't be allowed to live and inflict other people with his 'depressions'. Conan, who had immediately picked up on his master's mood, lay close by his side, keeping his breathing even to try and bring some comfort. As the mists swirled around inside his head, voices kept pummelling away at his conscience – end it all; you are a useless excuse for a human being; nobody loves you – round and round the voices went until he believed every word.

His pills were no longer kept in his bedside drawer, Meabh had insisted they were kept in the medicine cabinet in the bathroom so he wasn't tempted to take too many. He needed them now but it was just too much effort to put his legs over the side of the bed and stand up. He had given in to the darkness that overwhelmed him. Nothing, no one, could bring him out of this one. This was as bad as it got and if the pills couldn't help, then what could?

He heard the creak of the stairs, unaware what time it was. He cringed. He didn't want to see anyone. No one should have to see him like this. He pulled the pillow over his head and pushed his face into the mattress. Maybe if he pulled hard enough on the pillow he would suffocate and not have to put up with this any longer.

'Findlaech.'

A gentle voice tried to break through the barrier which was stopping any logical reasoning.

'Findlaech.'

There, he heard it again.

He thought he felt Conan leave the bed, but he couldn't be sure. In fact he couldn't be sure of anything. He wouldn't have been sure that he was still alive except for the pounding in his head.

'Findlaech, lad, it's your Da.'

He felt a warm hand placed in the centre of his back. It should have bought comfort. Any other day it would, but today he had slipped too far into the depths of despair.

Riley knew it was bad when he got no response. They had coped with several bad days, but none like this. He knew he needed Meabh's help.

'Ma, I need you,' he called down the stairs.

Meabh felt the hairs rise on the back of her neck. Surely they weren't too late were they? She dropped the tea towel, took off her apron and took the stairs two at a time.

As soon as she reached the bedroom door Riley met her with an expression that said it all. 'Oh, Da, not again.'

She went over to the bed, sat down on the side of the

mattress and gently prised his hands off the pillow. Gently, gently, was the only way to handle his moods. No quick moves, no loud sounds, no bright lights, just patience and love would hopefully break through.

'Son, we are here for you. See if you can turn over.'

It was then that the tears started. He didn't want to hurt the two people he loved, but he could no longer live this way. He hammered his fists into the mattress and allowed the tears to fall.

'I can't do it any more, Ma. I can't stand the pain. I can't stand the dark. Please make it go away.'

'Does your head hurt, son?' she asked gently, knowing what pattern these moods took.

In between sobs he managed to nod his head, but he still wouldn't turn over and look at her.

'Go into the bathroom and fetch his pills and those strong painkillers the neurologist gave us,' she said to Riley in her quiet, calm voice.

She turned back to Findlaech. 'We need to get rid of the physical pain first before we can break through your mental anguish, son. Will you take some pills for me, *please*. We love you so much and we can't possibly survive without you. You are our world now.'

At first the words would not break through the barrier he had built to protect himself. However, the more she spoke, the clearer his head became and he could see a chink of light breaking through the dark. The mists started to swirl as if a tornado were sending them round and round in his brain, but instead of black they were now turning grey.

Riley returned with a cup of tea and the two bottles of pills. He took two out from each bottle and handed them over to Meabh.

'Now son, please take these for me. We need to get rid of that pain.'

He slowly turned over but avoided looking Meabh in the face. He didn't want her to see his anguish. But Meabh didn't need to see his face to know that it would mirror the inner struggle he was fighting.

She gently stroked his hair back from his damp forehead. His whole body was drenched in sweat. 'Can you get me a cold flannel please?' she asked Riley in little more than a whisper.

She eventually coaxed Findlaech up into a sitting position and watched as he swallowed the four pills. She told him to lie back down with the pillow behind his head this time and she soothingly wiped over his closed eyes, across his forehead, down his cheeks, with the ice cold flannel.

Findlaech was only partially aware that anyone else was in the room. He started to sense a stroking movement over his face, cool, damp, soothing away the pain that hammered inside his brain. He allowed the motion to take over and gradually his stiffened limbs started to relax. As he took deep breaths the physical pain started to recede. The mental anguish too was being washed away with each movement of the flannel over his face. As he allowed his body and mind to sink into oblivion, he felt relaxed enough to fall asleep.

As soon as Meabh became aware of his deep breathing and the relaxed state of his body, she stopped massaging his face and stood up.

'We need to leave him now, Da, I think shopping might have to wait for another day. Today he will need his rest,' and she closed the bedroom door behind them.

They tiptoed downstairs. Conan, who had gone quickly out into the yard, returned and lay obediently down by his side. He synced his breathing with that of his master's until they were as one. He would never leave his side until he knew he was all right.

Findlaech slept soundly until one o'clock. He slowly opened his eyes afraid of how he might feel. The pain in his head had gone and he wasn't afraid of the strip of sunlight that played across his bed. He sat up slowly, stroking Conan to reward him for his loyalty. He gingerly put his legs over the side of the bed and stood. The world was still, the world was quiet, there were no voices in his head and he breathed a sigh of relief.

He went slowly downstairs and found Meabh sitting darning a pair of socks using the light from the window. She looked up as he approached, pleased to see his face showed no sign of stress and she gave him the biggest smile. She always took it slowly after one of his 'episodes', that was the way it had to be. She had learnt over the months how to handle each situation as it arose.

'Something to eat, son?'

Findlaech nodded.

'I'm going to take a bath, but I could murder some scrambled eggs on toast.'

Findlaech knew there was no need to say sorry, or thank you for that matter, they had an understanding. They would always be there for each other no matter how hard it got. Meabh was a very special person and one he had come to adore as if she were his own mother.

Riley came in at that point for his lunch and was relieved to see Findlaech up and about. He wasn't quite so good at hiding his emotions as his wife and he ran to Findlaech and gave him the biggest man hug.

'Now, now, Da, leave him be. He doesn't need all that smothering,' she said, but in the nicest possible way.

After lunch Riley asked Findlaech what he would like to do that afternoon.

'I've done all the day to day chores on the feirme, so the afternoon is free.'

Meabh was about to say he shouldn't exert himself, but Findlaech beat her to it. 'Can we still go shopping? I really want to see you poshing it up in a new outfit.'

She was about to say she didn't think it was wise, but then she thought about it and decided if that was going to make him happy then she shouldn't put a spanner in the works.

'Off you go and have your bath, lunch will be on the table when you are finished.'

The shopping trip was exactly what was needed. Riley wouldn't let Findlaech drive because of the drugs he had taken, but he was more than happy to be a passenger. The thought of shops a few months ago would have put the fear of God into him, but anything he did with Meabh and Riley turned out to be fun.

The department store Henry Lyons & Co. in Aclare offered them everything they needed, providing a good choice of both men and women's fashion. Although Meabh disagreed at first, Findlaech wanted her to try on a new outfit first, after which they would visit the men's department and she could give her opinion. It was agreed and between them they went through the rails picking out dresses, skirts, blouses, cardigans and even a pair of jeans – something she would never have considered wearing before. The two men sat patiently outside the dressing room and waited for Meabh to come out wearing a new ensemble.

'Oh, I can't believe it, this is actually too big for me!' she exclaimed. Pulling the waistband on the skirt and showing there was at least two inches to spare. 'Could you get me a smaller size please?'

After about thirty minutes she had chosen a dress, a new skirt, a pair of denim jeans and several tops. She took them up to the counter with pride. She had always made her own clothes because she would have been too embarrassed to ask for anything in her old size. Today was a revelation and she felt like a million dollars.

'Ma, while we look at men's clothes why don't you go into the hairdressers and have a new hairdo?' Riley said, pointing to a sign advertising a modern salon on the top floor.

If he had said that to her several months ago she would have asked what was wrong with her hair as it was, but because she was feeling so good about herself she took it just the way he meant it – as a special treat, not because she needed improving. She smiled. 'What a fabulous idea.'

So for the next hour they parted company.

Riley and Findlaech were only too happy to go through all

the choices of clothing until the dressing room was bursting with items for him to try on. Even Riley picked out a couple of new things because he said his trousers kept falling down.

Afterwards the two men had time to go to the top floor to the café and have a couple of coffees, from where they could see Meabh laughing and joking with the stylist in the salon opposite.

'You know son, I have never seen her this happy even when Niamh lived at home. We make a great threesome.' He held up his coffee cup and chinked it with Findlaech's, 'And long may it last.'

'I suspect you'll want to go home eventually, though,' Findlaech said with dread in his heart. He couldn't imagine life any other way now.

'Ah, we were going to talk to you about that.'

Findlaech's heart sank. He really didn't know how he would manage without them now. They had become his world, his soul mates and to all intents and purposes his parents. He could feel his good mood draining away and feared another episode of 'depressions' was on its way.

Riley immediately picked up on his reaction and spoke quickly. 'Aw, lad, don't look like that. It's nothing bad, I just don't want to talk about something with Ma now she is better.'

Findlaech was not convinced but tried to act normally. After all he had no right to expect them to live with him forever.

They all met down in the foyer at five o'clock as arranged. Meabh swayed down the stairs, wearing one of the new dresses, her hair cut in a modern bob, accentuated by a few highlights which lifted her features and made her look ten years younger.

'Ma, you look amazing,' Findlaech said. Riley was too stunned to speak. He definitely had a new wife.

'Son, I feel amazing,' she said hooking her arms into theirs as they sauntered out of the shop as if they didn't have a care in the world.

Except Findlaech did have a care. Findlaech had a major worry. How was he going to cope living on his own after the wonderful time he had spent with these two amazing human beings. He was exceptionally quiet all the way home which concerned Meabh. She was unaware that Riley had told him they needed to talk.

14 The Revelation

When they arrived home, the first thing Meabh asked was for Findlaech to show her what he had bought. He took them out of the bags and held them up one at a time.

"No, son, I want to see you showing them off. Go and put them on and pretend you are a model on the catwalk," she said laughing.

Findlaech, who still had a feeling of dread in the pit of his stomach, forced a smile. "I will, Ma, but first Riley told me there was something you wanted to tell me and I need to hear it now before I go mad."

"There's lots we have to say but it will wait until we all sit down to dinner. First, I want to see you in all your glad rags."

He knew he wouldn't win if she had her mind set on something so he reluctantly agreed. He took his purchases up to his bedroom and put on the new trousers, shirt, v-neck jumper and beautiful brown lace-up shoes instead of his normal dirty trainers. He looked quickly in his wardrobe mirror to make sure he looked all right and then went downstairs.

"Oh, son, don't you look the part," Meabh said clapping her hands together. "Mind you I think you should have come in the hairdressers with me because your fringe is hanging over your eyes."

"You've gone and spoilt it now, Ma. The boy looks fantastic and he doesn't need a haircut unless he wants one," Riley said in his defence.

Findlaech ran his fingers through his thick, blond locks and decided perhaps he would visit a barbers in the morning. He wanted to look good for his first night of dancing after all.

After he had changed out of his new clothes, the two men sat outside the back door drinking a stout before dinner. Findlaech still couldn't shake the feeling that they were about to deliver bad news, but tried not to let it show.

Meabh had treated them all to a lovely piece of sirloin steak while they were in town and, together with some potatoes dug up from the garden and a lovely fresh salad; it was a fitting meal for the news they were about to impart.

They had only eaten a couple of mouthfuls when Findlaech asked what it was they wanted to tell him.

"You're impatient, son, hold your horses," Riley said. He knew he was teasing but what he was about to tell him would either be good news to him or bad.

"Firstly," Meabh said, "we are going to be grandparents. Niamh phoned us last night to tell us the good news."

"That's fantastic news." Findlaech held up is glass and said, "Let's drink to the baby."

It was fantastic news but he still couldn't think straight because he knew that wasn't the only news they wanted to tell him. He was pretty certain now that they would want to go back to their own home, especially as there would be a new addition to the family. After all his cottage was small and there wasn't a spare room for their family to stay even if they wanted to. He suddenly went off his dinner.

"And?" he said.

"And? What do you mean 'and'?"

"That's not the only news is it. Please get it over with because I don't think I can bear it if you hang it out any longer."

Meabh looked at Riley and Riley looked at his wife. They hadn't expected him to see it this way and they could see it was upsetting him.

"Out with it, Da, before he has one of his turns," Meabh said laughing.

"I don't think it's a laughing matter," Findlaech said unable to look them in the face. "I have got so used to you living here I am not sure I can bear it when you leave."

Again Meabh and Riley looked at one another.

They both smiled.

"That answers the question for us then. We weren't sure how you were going to take our next piece of news."

Findlaech stood up and started pacing the kitchen. "How did you expect me to take it. Everyone I love walks out on me and now I am losing me Ma and Da for a second time." He simply couldn't stop the tears this time and Meabh stood and took him in her arms.

"Silly boy. Why don't you listen to what we have to say. I think you have the wrong end of the stick," Riley tried to explain. "My cousin came to us last week and asked if we would consider selling our feirme to him because he loves it so much. I couldn't give him an answer because we didn't know how you would feel about us living here permanently."

Findlaech's face was a picture. He just stood frozen in the middle of the kitchen, the pained expression already leaving his face.

"With the extra money, with your permission of course, we

thought we could extend your cottage a bit and make room for Niamh and her new family when they want to come and stay. It also means that if you and Clodagh stay seeing each other, it would give you a bit more space for entertaining."

Findlaech sat down again and immediately started tucking into his steak dinner.

"Well, why didn't you say before. It's marvellous news. It's the best news I have ever heard, apart from Ma losing all the weight that is, it's simply marvellous."

"And that's not all, Findlaech," Riley said pushing an envelope across the table.

"What's this? It looks suspiciously like a tax return by the colour of the envelope," Findlaech said suspiciously.

"Open it, son," Meabh said with the biggest smile on her face.

Slowly he opened the envelope not at all certain what he was going to find. Inside was a single sheet of paper with a crest and the words CERTIFICATE OF ADOPTION across the top of the page. He swallowed hard, unable to speak as the tears flowed down his face.

"Is this really true?" he eventually managed to say.

"Yes, Findlaech, you are now officially our son. Mind you they took a lot of persuading because of your age, but because of your circumstances they eventually gave way."

After much hugging and not to mention more tears, they all raised their glasses and made a toast to their new futures – together.

15 Clodagh

Clodagh Mary Quinn had not had the best start to life but she had, for the most part, been a happy child. School had been tough, the other kids tended to call her names and she only had one true friend, Niamh Ceallaigh, who looked out for her and wasn't afraid to stand up against the bullies. Clodagh found it hard to concentrate in lessons, her mind always drifting, so when she was asked a question she often just looked blankly at the teacher causing the other pupils to giggle.

Even though the teacher reprimanded them for being mean, it didn't help outside of school when they would tease her for having red hair, for being stupid, or for saying the wrong things. Even though the unkind words made her cry, she didn't dwell on it and tried to make the best of life. Because of the constant taunting she had become withdrawn, totally reliant on her parents, using drawing as a tool to express herself. She would draw all the animals on the feirme, the beautiful scenery which surrounded them and the birds that settled on the feeder outside her bedroom window. When her drawings became dark and sombre, her parents instinctively knew she was suffering an internal turmoil and they would take her to visit Doctor Fairleigh, under whose care she had been since the age of five. He understood how Clodagh's brain worked, how she assessed situations and taught her ways of handling them. The Quinns called him their 'miracle worker', but he was a modest man who told them he loved his job and wanted to see all his children live life to the fullest. He had become a close family friend over the years and never forgot Clodagh's birthday. Although an extremely busy man he always had time to talk and advise the Quinns.

Clodagh desperately wanted to fit in, desperately wanted to be liked, but her brain didn't work the same as other children's, or that is what the doctor had told her. She had been in and out of hospital for the first ten years of her life and this put her behind all the other kids. There was no special school for her to attend and so her parents had told her to 'just do your best'. She did try to do her best but it seemed her best was never quite good enough. At fifteen she asked her Ma and Pa if she could leave school and work with them on the feirme. At first they didn't like the idea, but the more they talked it over the more sense it made. Her affinity with animals helped greatly when handling the pigs and she quickly learned all her parents' skills. There was no need for exams or pieces of paper for Clodagh to prove her worth and as she became a young adult she fitted comfortably in her own skin and started to find her feet.

The day at the market when Findlaech had smiled at her had given her a strange sensation in her stomach. It was a nice feeling, like something was fluttering inside trying to get out. Apart from the young farmhands that worked with her parents, Clodagh had very little to do with men but she was drawn to returning his smile. She had never really thought about making new friends since Niamh had married. She had been with her parents to visit a couple of times, but she knew her friend had moved on to lead an adult life and Clodagh didn't know how to slot in any more. She felt like a book that had been pushed out of alignment on a shelf so she withdrew even more and rarely left her home.

Her drawings had become more elaborate and detailed as she got older but with little contact with the outside world the stresses had gone away and there was no need to put her frustration down on paper.

The evening after she met Findlaech she drew a person for the very first time. She drew from memory the striped awning, the trestle tables laden with produce and the man with the shock of blond hair chatting comfortably as he spoke to customers from inside his market stall. He had been so engrossed he hadn't noticed that he was being studied. Had he known he would have been self-conscious and uncomfortable. Because he was unaware, Clodagh was able to draw him exactly as she saw him, a confident, handsome young man.

She wasn't sure why she felt drawn to him. There was something about him that wasn't like anyone else. She knew from her parents that he had lost his Ma and his only brother and that for many years he had become a recluse. Perhaps because of this she could relate to him. Whatever the reason she did feel comfortable with him. When he had asked her Pa if he could take her for a lemonade her heart fluttered a little. Normally she wouldn't have been able to cope with talking to a stranger, but somehow she felt drawn to him and allowed him to take control of the situation. He was gentle, patient and she had no fear of him.

Their first date had been one of the best days of her life. She had never let anyone touch her, apart from her parents, but when Findlaech took her hand in the cinema it felt right. It didn't feel strange or uncomfortable and she allowed her body to relax and take strength from him. She didn't feel out of place, she didn't feel excluded, and as she sat with her hand in his she believed she could achieve anything.

Now she was going to go to a dance. She was excited. She was more than excited. The only time she had been dancing was at Niamh's wedding, and then she had to be coaxed out of her seat by her friend. She felt self-conscious at first but when Niamh told her to relax and let the music take over her body, she experienced something special. She felt like she was floating high above the other people. She watched herself, as the beat of the music allowed her to move her legs and arms freely. For once she didn't care what other people thought, all she wanted to do was dance and allow the music to take her to another place. Music became a calming factor and whenever she felt stressed she would put on a pair of headphones and become engrossed.

Because that day had been so special she told her Ma that she wanted to wear the same dress. They had bought it specially for the wedding and it was the prettiest shade of turquoise, with a flouncy skirt and handmade lace around the collar. She felt so good when she looked in the mirror and saw her auburn curls falling over her shoulders. She had never allowed herself to look properly at her reflection, scared of what might be looking back at her, but today, the day of the dance, she *did* look and she liked what she saw.

16 Light on His Feet

Findlaech was walking on air. The fact that Riley and Meabh weren't about to move out had been the best news he had ever received. The thought of life without them now seemed unbearable. Just the idea that this was what they wanted and that they saw him as their son did more to lift his spirits than any little blue pills from a bottle. He jumped out of bed the morning of the dance ready to take on the world. He couldn't explain why he felt so different that particular morning, but he did. He wanted to shout out and tell the world that he was really happy, but instead he ruffled Conan's head and ran downstairs to the smell of bacon.

"Bacon, Ma? A bit extravagant this morning," he said giving her the biggest kiss on her cheek.

"Yes, lad, we are celebrating, but I have cut off the fat and used the grill instead of frying."

"What are we celebrating?" he asked, knowing full well.

"The rest of our lives, son, the rest of our lives."

Findlaech grabbed her by the arms and swung her around. "You and Da are simply the best people in the world," he said laughing.

"Stop you fool, I'm getting giddy," she said in a mock scold, but she couldn't hide the smile reflected in her eyes. "Sit down breakfast is ready."

Findlaech talked nonstop through breakfast about all the plans he had for the feirme. A lot of the work they could do themselves, but for the extension they would need the help of a local builder, Patrick Ryan.

Riley spread pieces of paper all over the table while Meabh cleared away the dishes and the two men drew crude plans of what they had discussed. Meabh had never seen her husband so animated about anything and she felt a warm glow spread through her body.

Something had definitely been missing from their lives since Niamh had moved out. Because of this their health had suffered; Meabh had started to overeat to compensate and Riley just worried constantly about his wife and the feirme with no one to take over if anything happened to him. However, the gods had looked kindly on them and given them the son they so desperately wanted. Findlay may not be flesh and blood but to them he was and Niamh had taken to him as if he had been her true brother.

Meabh couldn't but help smile as she watched her two men discussing their future. She smoothed down her apron and started to wash up the breakfast dishes. Once she would have had to reach to turn the tap on due to her oversized belly, now she could reach with ease. She felt so good and her heart skipped a happy beat.

When evening came they waited with anticipation while Findlay got ready for the dance. As he walked down the stairs their eyes turned and he saw their faces light up with appreciation. Riley let out an enormous wolf whistle, while Meabh clapped her hands with joy.

"You are a sight for sore eyes, me lad," she said.

"Don't go overboard, Ma, it's just a suit."

"Just a suit! Have you taken a real good look at yerself in the mirror. You cut a fine figure of a man that any girl would be proud to be seen with."

She got up and gave him one of her hugs.

"Now, Ma, don't you be goin' and crumplin' his clothes," Riley said, giving Findlaech a pat on the shoulder. "But I have to agree you brush up well. Now, if you are ready let's be goin'."

They bounced up the lane in the old truck, kicking up dust behind them.

"You know what, son, I think we could afford a new truck. What do you say?"

"I think before you rush into anything we ought to see how much the extension costs. You know how everything seems to cost double what you expect," Findlaech said, erring on caution.

"You are right. I know you are right. And you will have to be the one in charge of the funds, son. You see I am rubbish with money, it has always been Ma who has kept me in tow."

"Well, I've never had any real money to be extravagant with so I guess that has taught me to be frugal. We will all talk things over before we buy anything and that way we won't waste money on things we don't really need."

"Sensible words, son, sensible words . . . Aw, will you look at that as pretty as a picture."

Clodagh was framed in the doorway, a shawl round her shoulders, wearing a smile that stretched for a mile or more. Her hair was loose and the curls bounced freely from her shoulders. She wore the faintest trace of lipstick and a hint of blue powder on her eyelids; she was as pretty as any painting Findlaech had ever seen.

As soon as the truck stopped, he jumped down and went and took her arm, first giving her the lightest of kisses on her cheek.

"Your carriage awaits, Cinderella," Riley said.

"Sorry, it's not exactly a carriage, but we can use our imagination," Findlaech said laughing.

Clodogh should have been nervous. She had been nervous and excited all day and had been unable to eat a thing, but as soon as she sat down beside Findlaech and felt the warmth of his leg against her thigh, she relaxed.

"It's a carriage to me," she said, "and the two men inside are my princes."

This caused both men to laugh.

Their laugh was infectious and Clodagh joined in.

"You know what, I don't think I have really laughed in years. Tonight is going to be such fun," she said resting her hand gently on Findlaech's arm.

Findlaech had expected her to be a bit quiet and on edge, but he was pleasantly surprised to see how at ease she was. "Yes, tonight is going to be such fun, as long as I don't tread on your toes!"

"You will be fine, Findlaech. Ma, has taught you well," Riley said as they drew up outside the village hall.

Findlaech just smiled, jumping down and lifting Clodagh down from the cab.

"I'll be back at eleven to pick you two lovebirds up," Riley said, whistling as he drove away down the high street.

The village hall had been transformed, with bunting hanging from the beams, round the windows, across the front of the stage and subtle lighting giving it an almost surreal atmosphere. There were tables and chairs placed around a central dance floor which was already full of couples girating and swirling to the band now in full swing on the stage. Clodagh was entranced, and looked around her. She never dreamt that one day she would come to a dance, let alone with the man of her dreams.

Findlaech brought her out of her thoughts by guiding her to a free table.

"Sit down while I go and get us a couple of drinks. What would you like?"

"The only alcoholic drink I have ever tried was a Babycham one Christmas, but the bubbles tickled my nose and I am not sure I really liked the taste."

"Then why don't you have something you do like. I shall have a beer if that is all right, but you have a drink you like the taste of."

Clodagh felt relieved he hadn't pushed her into having a real drink and asked him for a lime juice and soda.

"Perfect," he said. "Won't be a minute."

Clodagh watched the people dancing, enjoying every minute of it. The throbbing of the base notes vibrated up the legs of her chair and made her tap her feet. She loved music. She loved dancing. She was taking part in her very own fairytale.

Findlaech watched her face as he walked back to the table carrying their drinks. He could see the excitement in her eyes, the rhythm of her foot tapping against the chair leg and he found it hard to believe that he was the same person who over a year ago had hardly dared to venture out of the front door.

He couldn't be certain what she would say when it came to the time for discussing his 'depressions', but tonight he was going to enjoy himself, laughing and dancing with the most beautiful girl in the room.

"It was difficult not to spill it with all the people jostling up against the bar," he said as he placed the tall glass down in front of Clodagh.

"It is very busy isn't it."

"Are you all right with all these people?" he asked thoughtfully.

"Oh yes, I don't even see them. All I can hear is the music and you, of course," she added turning to give him the most enchanting smile. "Can we dance?"

Findlaech felt his stomach tighten slightly at the word 'dance', but that is what they had come for and all he had to do was remember Meabh's words of encouragement.

He stood up, took her hand in his and said, "Shall we go to the ball, princess?"

"Oh, Findlaech, you are so funny and thank you for putting me at ease."

They stayed on the edge of the dance floor so as not to get bumped by the other couples already swaying to the music. Findlaech remembered his Ma's words, took Clodagh's hand in his and placed his other hand gently on her back. At first he was a little stiff and found it hard to take the lead.

"Let me be the man, so to speak, just follow my feet," Clodagh said encouragingly into his ear, aware that he was feeling a little anxious. Normally she would have been too shy, but whatever magic Findlaech had inside him had rubbed off on her.

Findlaech nodded and as she guided him round the dance floor, encouraging him with every step, he gradually started to relax and let the beat and the intoxicating closeness of her body take over his movements. He followed her every lead; one foot forward, one foot back, one step to the side and then spin around. As he got used to the steps he found it totally exhilarating and they danced until he eventually had to tell her he needed a drink.

Clodagh nodded and he led her back to the table. A little flushed and out of breath, they both sat down, looked at each other and burst out laughing.

"Findlaech, I was so nervous about tonight, and yet here we are like two old friends, dancing the night away." She held up her glass and chinked it against his. "Thank you," she mouthed silently.

"No, thank you, Clodagh. I am having the very best time."

"You know, once you learned to relax, you really are very light on your feet."

"That's a compliment I never thought I'd hear."

He leaned across the small table and bravely placed his lips very gently on hers. She responded by putting her hands on his shoulders and pulling him a little closer.

It was the perfect end to a more than perfect night.

17 Brick Dust and Cakes

Findlaech and Clodagh had a regular date night every Friday when he would either take her to the cinema, out for something to eat and, once a month, return to the dance at the village hall.

Once a year Clodagh had an appointment with Doctor Fairleigh to check on her progress and also have a blood test to ensure the medication was the correct dose to prevent further seizures.

"Ma, I would like Findlaech to take me to the hospital if that is all right with you."

Mrs Quinn was taken aback by this sudden change to routine, but then she shouldn't have been surprised as over the past few months her daughter had transformed from a shy, damaged young girl into a beautiful, confident young woman.

"Of course, darling, if that is what you would like, it is fine with us."

"Thank you, Ma," said Clodagh giving her mother a big hug.

This, again, was something so out of character, as her daughter had always shied away from physical contact even as a young child. Once when she had grazed her knee falling off a seesaw, she had curled up in a foetal position and refused to accept any comforting. She knew the change was mostly, possibly totally, due to Findlaech. He himself had undergone a miraculous transformation from a shy, reclusive character into a young man who was brimming with confidence. It was nothing short of a miracle that two people had overcome such major obstacles in their early lives. Findlaech must be an exceptional young man, she thought, for she had also seen the transformation to Meabh. She had always worried for her friend due to her obesity and now here she was a slim, happy and fit woman taking life in her stride. Once a week she would cycle to have tea with Mrs Quinn and all she ever talked about was her family and how happy they all were. Yes, a miracle, indeed.

Findlaech had passed his driving test first time, but then it wasn't hard in Aclare because the roads were so quiet. He arrived home, flushed, grinning and waving the certificate in their air. All three had jumped about the kitchen causing Conan to start barking and rushing round the kitchen table like a mad thing. He always picked up on their excitement. In fact he was so excited he grabbed one of Meabh's furry slippers from in front of the Aga and ran out of the back door with it.

"Da, he's got me slipper. He'll cover it in slobber."

Both men ran out of the back door still laughing and chased Conan across the yard. Needless to say he jumped the gate, believing it to be a game, and ran across the meadow with the slipper still tightly gripped between his teeth.

"Conan! Conan! Get back here this minute!" Findlaech yelled.

Goliath also picked up on the excitement and charged the gate, which they had left unlatched, and ran across the meadow after Conan. Meabh stood in the back door watching the mayhem. She couldn't be angry. She was never angry these days, life was simply too perfect. In fact it was such a funny sight seeing a dog, followed by a goat, followed by two grown men that she started to laugh so much she got a stitch.

Conan was having such fun he wasn't listening to the voices shouting behind him. Aware that Goliath was also chasing him, he made it into even more of a game by stopping occasionally, turning around and taunting the goat with the slipper. He ran and ran, forgetting about the section of marshy ground in the far corner of the paddock. There had been several days of rain and, although today was bright and sunny, the ground in that corner was miry. He knew his mistake as soon as he stood on it and his feet started to sink into the gloopy mud which was covered in a bright, almost velvety-looking moss disguising what was below. Deeper and deeper he sunk, the panic starting to show in his eyes.

Goliath stopped himself in time and let out a sorrowful bleat as he watched Conan disappearing before his eyes. He tried to get closer but as soon as he felt the soft ground he backed up and bleated again.

Findlaech and Riley also stopped on the edge of the bog, hands on hips, staring at Conan. Findlaech put a hand on Goliath's horn and pulled him back, "No, we don't want two of you stuck. We'll get him out."

"I knew we should have made fencing the bog a priority," Riley said.

"How deep do you think it is?" Findlaech asked.

"You tell me, lad. You'd better run back and get a rope before he sinks completely, don't you think. Us standing here and gawping ain't going to help him."

Findlaech turned on his heels and sprinted back across the

meadow. That wayward dog had saved his life on a couple of occasions and he wasn't about to lose him now. Luckily, Meabh had already pre-empted the predicament and was making her way across the meadow carrying a coil of rope.

"Couldna' have done that a year ago," she said, slightly breathless but exhilarated by the fact she could now run.

"Thanks, Ma."

Findlaech ran back to where Riley was standing, giving encouragement to Conan. Although his eyes showed fear, he had the sense to remain totally still which slowed his descent into the bog.

"If you lay down on your stomach I'll hang onto your legs," Riley said.

Findlaech carefully felt the ground in front of him and lay himself down until he could reach Conan's head.

"You stay still, old chap, while I put this round your neck. Stay still you hear me."

Conan looked into his eyes, placing all his trust in his master. He remained perfectly still while Findlaech put the rope around his neck. Scared he would strangle him if they pulled hard, he pushed his hands into the cloying mud and managed to get the rope behind his front legs, forming a loop.

He then edged his way gently off the bog and, with the help of Riley, was about to start pulling when Goliath nudged him in the back, bleating loudly.

"You know, I think he wants to help," Findlaech said. "I am going to tie the rope around his horns and hopefully the three of us will have enough strength to pull Conan out.

They tugged and tugged and tugged until slowly Conan's

body started to emerge. As soon as he was on firm ground he shook from head to tail splattering everyone in the dark, peaty mud.

They looked a right sight as they all trudged back across the meadow covered from head to toe in detritus.

"I suppose I'll need to treat myself to a new pair of slippers, then," Meabh said, without a trace of anger in her voice.

No one had noticed throughout the fiasco that Conan still had the slipper firmly gripped between his teeth.

"Will you look at that, Ma. He never let go!"

Conan, looking sufficiently apologetic, placed the slipper into Meabh's hand. Despite the fact that every part of him was plastered in mud, she patted him on the top of the head and said, "I forgive you, Conan, but if you ever pull a stunt like that again, it's the shed for you!"

He wagged his tail, jumped up and placed his feet on her chest, leaving two lovely muddy footprints. "Get off you stupid mutt," but she still had a smile on her face.

They had a fight as to who would have the first bath that night.

At dinner, having recovered from their dirty exploits, Meabh turned to Findlaech and asked, "Do you think Clodagh would like to come to tea one afternoon?"

"Do you know, Ma, I think it would be an excellent idea. We are going to the hospital on Friday so why don't we come here afterwards."

"What a lovely idea and I will make a spread fit for a princess."

"Of that I have no doubt, your teas are simply the best."

Findlaech soon realised that driving his girlfriend around in the old farm truck wasn't really ideal. Riley had seen an advert in the local shop for a Mini which, although twelve years old, only had around 25,000 miles on the clock. He pointed it out to Findlaech and the pair went off to check it out. It was only about 22 miles from their place and when they arrived they were pleasantly surprised to find the car had been the old man's pride and joy and had always been kept under cover. He lifted off the tarpaulin, which although a little dusty, revealed an immaculate pale blue Mini underneath.

Mr Parrish handed Findlaech the key and told him to have a drive to see if he liked the way she handled. Findlaech loved the fact that he had given the car a gender, he knew then that it had been well cared for.

They took it for a drive around the local roads and the engined purred like a satisfied pussy cat.

When they arrived back at the house, Mr Parrish asked, "Well, what do you think?"

"I think she is perfect, Mr Parrish, and I would be proud to be the new owner of your car," Findlaech replied.

Riley had drawn the cash out of the bank in case the car was satisfactory and handed Mr Parrish the envelope telling him that it was all there and could they have a receipt. He disappeared into his house and came back a few minutes later with a signed receipt, the log book and a grubby little ledger showing what work had been carried out on the car. They shook hands and sealed the deal.

Meabh was so excited when they arrived home and she clapped her hands with joy.

"Oh, don't get out, son, I want to go for a spin."

"Good job you lost all that weight, Ma, I don't think I could have squeezed you in before!!"

"Enough of your cheek, young man, I could still give you a good spanking." And, like everything they did these days, they laughed at the sheer exuberance of life.

Two days later Findlaech arrived to pick up Clodagh to take her to Sligo General Hospital for her appointment with Doctor Fairleigh. When she opened the door and saw the little blue Mini sitting outside the cottage she gave Findlaech the biggest hug.

"It's just the sweetest little car I have ever seen," she exclaimed.

Hearing the excitement in their daughter's voice the Quinns came out to see what it was all about.

"Well, that's a bit different from Riley's old truck," her father said, slapping Findlaech on the back.

Findlaech needed to pinch himself to make sure he wasn't living in a dream. Here he was leading a normal life, mixing with people and loving every minute of it. He still had his bad days, he knew they could never leave him completely, but he was coping and now he knew they always went away.

They drove to the hospital with Findlaech doing most of the talking. He told Clodagh that Patrick Ryan had made a start on digging the foundations for the extension and talked animatedly about the plans they had drawn up. "Oh, and Ma is so excited about you coming to tea, you should see what she has baked."

"You know, Findlaech, I would love to learn to bake. Do you think she would teach me?"

"I know she would be delighted, but what about your own mother, wouldn't she be upset?" Findlaech asked.

"Me Ma is a bit too busy with her work and I don't like to bother her."

Mrs Quinn had started a nursery for pre-school children in the local scout hut. It had become an instant hit with all the mums that wanted to go back to work, or were too busy with their farms to mind a toddler safely. It was tiring, but with the help of two local women, they managed to run a very successful business. The idea had been partly because Mrs Quinn had desperately wanted another child, but after the complications with Clodagh the doctors had advised on sterilisation. She had nearly lost her life in childbirth and she knew it was not worth the risk. Looking after children satisfied her maternal urges and had made her a far happier person.

On arrival at the hospital, Findlaech parked the Mini in the car park, collecting a ticket from the machine and making sure to put it safely in his top pocket. They sat in the waiting room outside the consultant's office talking about Conan's escapade into the bog with Meabh's slipper. When Doctor Fairleigh called out her name they were so busy laughing they didn't hear the first time. He walked a little closer and repeated her name, not believing what he was seeing. Could this possibly be the same Clodagh Quinn he had been treating for over twenty-two years?

"Clodagh?" he said.

"Oh, sorry, doctor. Findlaech here was telling me a very funny story."

Findlaech waited outside while Clodagh followed the doctor into his consulting room. "Can Findlaech come in too, please, doctor? There is nothing you could say that I wouldn't want him to hear," she assured him.

"Of course, please come in," he said pointing to the two chairs at the side of the room. He didn't like to sit behind his desk when he was seeing a patient, he liked to sit beside them as he had found this less intimidating.

He watched with interest as the pair took their seats. Had he not known better he could have sworn this was Clodagh's twin sister, she was so different. She had a sparkle in her eyes which before had always been lustless and tired. Her cheeks were flushed with pink like a perfect rose petal, where once they had been pale and dull. In all the years he had treated this young woman, not once had she managed to give him eye contact, she always looked at her hands which fiddled and fidgeted in her lap. Here she was, as bright as a button, looking him straight in the eye and actually laughing. What a transformation. He couldn't believe he had ever seen such a miracle in all his years as a doctor.

"Clodagh, I don't need to ask, I can see you are doing really well," he said without bothering to even open the file with her notes.

"Doctor Fairleigh, I feel on top of the world. I don't know what happened to me but from the day I met Findlaech here I just changed. I don't want to hide away any more, I want to live. I have been doing extra exercises on my arm and, look, I can even pick things up in my left hand now."

"Clodagh, that is absolutely wonderful news and I can't tell you how happy that makes me. All we need to do now is to take some blood just to make sure we have your level of medication right. Is that OK?"

"Yes, of course," and she started to roll up her sleeve. "Do you think I will ever be able to come off the pills, doctor?"

"I would like to say, yes, Clodagh, but I don't think it is worth the risk of you having a seizure. We can hopefully reduce the dose so it doesn't make you quite so sleepy, but let's see what the blood results tell us first."

"Oh, I'm not sleepy any more, doctor. I just have too much to do. I am going to tea at Findlaech's today and I am going to ask his Ma if she can help me bake. Also Findlaech has said I can help him with his animals when I am not too busy with the pigs."

Findlaech could see a slight look of confusion on the doctor's face, but wasn't quite sure what he was thinking. Perhaps he thought Clodagh was doing too much and was worried for her well-being. He was about to say he would make sure she didn't overdo it when the doctor spoke directly to him.

"Findlaech, correct me if I am wrong, but I believe your mother passed away when you were a young lad."

Findlaech wasn't sure where this had come from. Why would the doctor bring up his mother? He frowned, confusion furrowing his brow.

"It's just that Clodagh said your Ma was going to teach her to bake," the doctor clarified.

They both laughed.

"Me Ma did pass away, doctor, but Meabh and Riley Ceallaigh originally from Glen Beag Farm adopted me and now we are all living together at my place, Pound Field Farm."

This was a day of surprises and Doctor Farleigh stood up, shook Findlaech's hand and said it had been one of the best days in his years of doctoring. "You two are what makes my job worthwhile. You look after each other you hear me. I will ring you Clodagh when I have the blood results back and will let your GP know if we need to change the dose."

They both shook his hand and thanked him, walking out of the consulting room hand in hand. Another surprise for the doctor, aware that Clodagh had always hated any physical contact.

They drove back to the feirme, talking about all the things they knew Meabh would have baked – fruit scones, cheese scones, cheese straws, strawberry tarts, chocolate brownies, Victoria sponge filled with jam and fresh cream and, one of Findlaech's favourites, banana bread. Anything they didn't eat would be taken down to the children's home on the outskirts of Sligo to make sure Meabh wasn't tempted to eat too much sweet stuff.

When they arrived in the yard, Meabh was already waiting in the doorway, hands all floury and wiping them on her pretty floral apron.

"It's so lovely to see you Clodagh, do come in."

You could have knocked her down with a feather when Clodagh ran forward and gave Meabh a big hug.

"Thank you so much for inviting me, I am so excited," she said.

Meabh could also see a big change in the young woman. She was barely recognisable from that day in the market. She looked at Findlaech who was smiling from ear to ear and told them to go and sit down while she brewed some tea.

Riley came in from the paddock after completing the fencing around the boggy area, covered in mud. "Mind you take them boots off and go and wash your hands before tea," Meabh said.

"As bossy as ever is our Ma," said Riley, but everything was always said with a smile these days.

There was silence for a good twenty minutes while they all tucked into the array of sandwiches and delights all laid out on the kitchen table. Meabh had even put her best lace tablecloth out with a beautiful bunch of sweet peas in the centre.

Meabh passed a plate to Clodagh who held up her hand. "I honestly couldn't eat another thing, thank you Mrs Ceallaigh. It was all so delicious."

"Don't you think we ought to take a plate out to Patrick, Ma, I am sure he would appreciate it?" Riley suggested.

"Oh my goodness, Patrick. I forgot about Patrick. May I be forgiven," Meabh said, shocked that she had forgotten about the poor man slaving away outside.

She made up a tray of food with a big mug of hot steaming tea and took it round to the area that had become a building site at the back of the feirme.

"Patrick, we were having afternoon tea and I thought you might like a nibble," she said.

"A nibble, woman, that is more of a banquet," he said laughing. "Thank you very much, I'll take me break now and enjoy every mouthful."

When Meabh returned to the lounge the three of them

were chatting about the work being done to the farmhouse and again was surprised to see Clodagh joining in the conversation. The excitement in their voices about all the extra space they would have was infectious and Clodagh listened, taking in every detail. They continued chatting until there was a knock on the door. The door was already ajar and Patrick put his head round the corner of the frame to say he was returning his mug and plate.

"Did you enjoy your tea?" Riley asked. "My wife's a great baker isn't she. Not that she does it so much these days because we are all watching our waistlines."

"You can say that again, Riley, best afternoon tea of my life. With one exception!"

"You saying something was wrong with my baking?" Meabh asked with surprise in her voice.

"Oh no, Meabh, not at all. You see I was just eating my last two mouthfuls of Victoria sandwich when I dropped it. It was too tasty to waste, so I picked it up right quick and crunched me way through to the last tasty morsel."

"Crunched, you say?" Findlaech said in surprise.

"Yes, lad. That's the only way I can describe it. You see it was covered in brick dust and consequently my cake was a bit crunchy. Still a bloody good cake, though. Excuse me Irish."

Everyone burst out laughing, including Clodagh, who couldn't think of a time when she had ever felt so welcomed into a family.

18 Tinsel and Turkey

Findlaech's episodes of depression were certainly becoming less frequent and when they did hit him he had enough support from his family and Clodagh to make sure he didn't sink too deep into despair. Like Clodagh, he would have to stay on medication for the rest of his life, but it was a small price to pay for relative normality. Not once in the past year had his moods turned so dark that he didn't want to carry on, he now had far too much to lose. He had a Ma, a Pa, a half-sister, a girlfriend and also his very loyal dog.

At first Conan did not adjust well to his master's relationship with Clodagh and always tried to push his way in between them if they sat together on the sofa. But as he got to know Clodagh better and knew she was a soft touch where treats were concerned, he softened and let them both be his friends.

Once the extension was complete, Findlaech and his Da tackled the decorating, while Meabh made new loose covers for the sofa and chairs in the original snug. She also made new curtains and matching cushion covers, using bright and cheerful fabrics. Much of their own furniture which had been put into storage, now fitted into the new rooms and by Christmas the whole place was fit for a king. They now had a spare room in which Clodagh could stay when it got late and also a place for Niamh and her daughter, Cara, when they were visiting.

Meabh absolutely adored being a grandmother and spoilt Cara at every opportunity. The house was always a bustle of activity and laughter, a complete contrast to Findlaech's life after his mother died.

Their first Christmas together was like nothing Findlaech had ever experienced. The whole cottage was decorated from head to foot and the smells which kept wafting out of the kitchen made him salivate whenever he came inside. He came in with his cheeks glowing red from the winter chill. He had spent the last few hours outside with Riley erecting a new woodstore. It was Christmas Eve and when they sat down in the evening for their meal, Meabh said she had a surprise.

Findlaech had been a little disappointed he couldn't spend Christmas Day with Clodagh, but he knew she needed to be with her parents.

"It's only one day," Riley said, finishing his last mouthful of creamy mashed potato.

"I appreciate that, Da, but it would have been extra special if she could have spent it with us."

"I agree with Findlaech," Meabh said as she started clearing away the dishes. "Christmas is special and friends, families and loved ones should spend it together."

"Come on then, Ma, what's your surprise," Findlaech said, getting up to help with the dishes. "I think you have already surprised us plenty with that Christmas tree in the lounge. And, there are rather a lot of presents underneath it for just three people."

"My surprise," Meabh said beaming, "is that Clodagh and her parents are coming to spend Christmas Day with us."

"But what about Niamh, Frank and Cara, I thought you had promised they could come," Riley said a little taken aback.

"They are coming, but I thought it wouldn't be complete without Clodagh here and the only way to do that was to invite her parents as well."

"Where are you going to seat everyone?" Riley asked. "Have you really thought this through? And isn't it too much work for you?"

"So many questions, dear husband. So many questions."

"Well, I'm a little concerned it's all a bit too much."

"Don't be such a party pooper, Da, we will work it out and it will be so much fun," Meabh said, punching him gently on the chest. 'Clodagh has promised to help me cook. She is coming on a treat since her lessons with me.'

Findlaech had listened, but his mind was elsewhere. He was already making plans so they could fit everyone round the kitchen table.

"Can I leave the dishes tonight please, Ma, I have something I need to do."

They both looked as he grabbed his hat and coat, donned on his pair of lined boots and headed back out into the yard. Riley was about to follow, but Meabh stopped him saying that she thought he might like to be left alone. She had no idea what he was planning, but whatever it was she felt it was important.

They could hear a lot of banging, sawing and drilling coming from the workshop in the corner of the barn, but both bided their time and waited until Findlaech returned.

After about three hours he came into the kitchen rubbing his hands.

"I'd like some help now please, Da, if you don't mind."

They were both intrigued as to what Findlaech had been

doing outside in the barn and Riley put on his coat and boots and followed him outside.

They returned a few minutes later carrying a large table, one end of which had two legs and the other, two pieces of wood sticking out from underneath.

Findlaech could see from Meabh's frown that she was uncertain exactly what it was.

"Ma, it's a temporary extension to our current kitchen table. See, if you slip these two pieces of wood underneath the old tressle, we can screw them in place with these small screws and it will give us plenty of room for everybody."

"Ingenious, son, ingenious," Riley said slapping him on the back.

Christmas morning every one was up early. None of the presents under the tree had been touched; they were for after dinner when everyone was together.

Meabh had everything in control in the kitchen, so Riley and Findlaech went outside to see to the animals and give them an extra special breakfast. They hung a few bits of tinsel round the goats' necks, Conan had his own piece twisted round his leather collar and the hen and duck house had also been decorated with holly and tinsel. It was all so festive.

Their guests descended on the now extended Pound Field Farm at around midday, with armfuls of presents and boxes of chocolates, nuts, dates, chestnuts, marshmallows for toasting on the fire and loads of games.

Once they had all said hello, Findlaech took everyone's coats and Clodagh's hand so that she followed him out to the hall. He hung up the coats in the new cupboard that had been installed in the lobby for coats and shoes and then turned to Clodagh, took her beautiful face between his hands and then kissed her lips with so much tenderness it bought tears to her eyes.

"Merry Christmas my beautiful princess," he said.

She smelt so intoxicating he wanted to take her in his arms and never let her go.

"Happy Christmas my handsome prince," she said pulling him towards her again. "This is going to be the best Christmas I have ever had." She had a smile on her face like the Cheshire Cat from *Alice in Wonderland*.

When they got into the new lounge they watched as Cara was allowed to unwrap one of her presents to keep her amused while they all sat down to dinner. It was a small, brightly coloured spinning top, which spun round and round as you pumped the spindle on the top. Cara was delighted and sat on the floor bouncing up and down, clapping her hands and giggling. Her laughter was so infectious soon the whole room was joining in.

Riley retired to the kitchen to do his one food-related job – carve the turkey. He was busy making neat slices out of the huge breast when he noticed something sticking out from the rear orifice of the turkey.

"Meabh?" he called.

Meabh quickly joined him in the kitchen, still smiling at the antics of their granddaughter.

"Meabh, what on earth is this?" he asked as he started pulling and pulling at the protuberance. It seemed to go on and on.

Suddenly Meabh started laughing.

"Oh my goodness! So that's what happened to my missing piece of tinsel. I looked everywhere for it. I had it hanging round my neck when I made the stuffing and it must have dropped into the bowl."

"Oh you beautiful, crazy woman, I love you with every breath of my body," Riley said placing his rather greasy hands around her now extremely slender waist.

They sat down to their sumptuous feast at around two, starting off by pulling crackers and reading out the ridiculous jokes. This was followed by a seafood cocktail, then roast turkey with all the trimmings – minus the tinsel – and then of course, Meabh's famous Christmas pudding with brandy butter, cream or custard for those who preferred it.

They were still all laughing about the turkey and tinsel even after every scrap had been eaten.

Everyone was full to bursting and Findlaech sent everyone into the lounge, including his Ma and Pa, saying that he and Clodagh were going to clear up and there was to be no arguing.

Meabh wasn't going to argue, not only were her legs aching after all the standing, but she also knew that the youngsters could do with some time alone. She kissed them both on the cheek and then retired to put her feet up.

"We'll bring you some coffee when we're done," Clodagh said. "And thank you Meabh, you have made my Christmas."

Clodagh put on Meabh's apron and started washing up. Findlaech grabbed a tea towel and dried each item as she put it on the drainer and then put everything away in the cupboards so that the kitchen returned to some semblance of normality.

As he turned round from putting the roasting tin away, he watched Clodagh highlighted against the window frame and his heart leapt. He had never experienced such emotions and he found it hard not to rush over and hold her. Then he wondered why he needed to be restrained, she had never shied away from his affections. So he closed the cupboard door quietly, walked up quietly behind her while she was still occupied and put his hands around her waist. He parted her beautiful auburn hair and placed a kiss in the nape of her neck.

Clodagh didn't bother drying her hands and placed them over his, covering him in soap bubbles. Her eyes reflected the love she had for him and her smile would have made even the darkest room bright.

"I love it when you are spontaneous with me, Findlaech."

She spun around and started to kiss him with so much passion that Findlaech was finding it hard to control himself.

"Whoa, you better stop Clodagh!"

"Why, what have I done wrong?" She looked aghast as if she had been reprimanded.

"Nothing, nothing, my beautiful princess, it's just that I am not sure I can control myself if you keep kissing me like that."

Clodagh's face lit up and she started laughing.

"You are such a gentleman, Findlaech Doyle, and I love every inch of your body."

"Oh Clodagh, I am so relieved you feel the same way as I do. Do you think you could ever see yourself becoming my wife?" he asked nervously.

Time stood still as he watched her freeze. Had he gone too far too soon?

Then before he had any more time to doubt himself, she rushed forwards and kissed him as if it were the last kiss they would ever have. Neither wanted to let go and they stood there frozen in time.

"Oh, Findlaech, I didn't think this Christmas could get any better. Now you have given me the best present of my life."

He held her hands in his and kissed her palms gently.

"I appreciate we both have health issues, but if we look out for each other then hopefully they will become insignificant," Findlaech said. "We have some presents to open, so we better not keep them waiting any longer."

Clodagh made a huge pot of coffee, while Findlaech put cups and saucers, spoons, cream and sugar onto a tray.

They made their present opening last for over two hours by numbering each one of the presents. Riley had a book to say which number belonged to which person, and they took it in turns to pick a number out of a hat.

Because only one person could open their present at a time, it meant that each person appreciated what everyone else was receiving. It was an ingenious idea and one that they said they would carry on each year.

After Niamh had put Cara to bed, they all had a drink and started to play games. By twelve o'clock everyone was yawning so Mr Quinn said it was probably time he got Clodagh and her mother home before they fell asleep.

"Before you go, Clodagh and I have some news we want to tell you," Findlaech said standing up in the middle of the lounge.

Clodagh went and stood by his side and he took her hand.

"Today I asked Clodagh to become my wife and I am the luckiest man alive because she has said 'yes'. I apologise to Mr Quinn, because by rights I should have asked him first, but I have become an impetuous fool where Clodagh is concerned and I never want her out of my life."

There were lots of tears and hugs and kisses before the Quinn family departed for home.

As Meabh and Riley lay in bed, having just put out their bedside lights, she turned to her husband and said that it had quite simply been the best Christmas she had ever had.

19 Tubes and Tears

Winter with all its frost and snow was giving way to Spring. The last of the snow was melting and little green shoots were trying to reach the weak sunlight so they could grow with renewed strength. The animals were also enjoying the warmth of the sunshine on their backs after all the cold months.

Meabh stood at the kitchen window watching the world with a mug of coffee in her hand. Riley was enjoying the rare pleasure of reading the Sunday paper with a plate of hot buttered crumpets balanced on his knee. A trickle of melted butter trickled down his chin and he wiped it away with the cuff of his shirt.

Findlaech was getting ready to drive Clodagh into town to look at engagement rings. The roads had been too icy to risk driving there during the winter months, but neither cared, they were too happy. Clodagh knew exactly what she wanted – a single diamond set in a plain gold band – nothing fancy, she wasn't a fancy type of girl.

Findlaech came downstairs into the kitchen, followed by Conan, who very rarely let him out of his sight. He seemed to have a sixth sense where his master's moods were concerned, and would jump up and lick his face if he sensed he was having a bad time. Today, however, Findlaech was on top of the world and nothing was going to spoil it.

"Morning, Ma," he said going to the breadboard to slice himself a nice wedge of crusty wholemeal bread. Since Meabh had been on her diet she wouldn't allow white bread in the house. Nobody cared; Meabh's bread was so good.

"Want some scrambled egg on that?" she asked turning back from the window. "It's a glorious day."

"I can do it, Ma, I'm not helpless you know," he said with a smile.

She patted him gently on top of his head, "No, you're far from helpless, but I love to pretend you are still a child." She laughed and got a pan out of the drawer under the cooker.

"Are you excited?" she asked.

"Yes, I am, Ma. It's not every day you get to buy your princess a diamond ring. Never in my wildest dreams did I imagine this day would ever come."

"You both deserve it," Meabh said, plonking a motherly kiss on his cheek. "You have had tough times but together your future is bright."

"Oh, yes, as bright as the largest star in the sky," he said sitting down at the table.

Clodagh, who had also just finished breakfast, was sitting squeezing a rubber ball in her left hand. With her parents' and Findlaech's help she had done all the exercises the physio had given her to improve the use in her left arm. Today was an important day, and she needed her left arm to work. Today, Findlaech would be placing a ring on her left hand.

The doctor had been so pleased with the results of her blood test that he had said she could reduce the dose of her medication so long as she returned every month to have her blood tested in case there was a drastic change. Clodagh had agreed and was delighted to think that she was improving day by day. Just like Findlaech, she struggled some days with her mobility and the violent headaches which were all part and parcel of her disability. Today, however, she felt on top of the world and she was ready and waiting when Findlaech knocked on the door.

Neither of them were used to the hustle and bustle of town and Findlaech had to circle the car park a couple of times before he found a space for his little Mini. Luckily it was in a corner, because living in the country with so much space, he was worried it might get knocked here in the busy metropolis.

They walked hand in hand down the high street looking in the jewellers' windows. Clodagh couldn't see anything she really liked in the first two but when they went down one of the side streets and found a small, independent jewellers she clapped her hands in delight. There, right in the middle of the window, was her ring.

"Oh, that's the one, Findlaech," she said getting rather excited.

"Right, let's go inside and try it on," he said.

The little bell rang above the door and an elderly gentleman came from behind a curtain wearing a pair of double glasses. He removed the outer pair and welcomed the couple into his shop with a broad smile showing some rather decaying teeth.

"We would like to try the ring in the centre of your window please," Findlaech said. "I can show you if you like."

"Thank you, perhaps you could point it out to me," the man said.

He carefully lifted the card out of the window which was

beautifully cushioned in dark blue velvet. Right in the middle was a slim platinum ring with a single diamond set in the centre.

The smile on Clodagh's face was a picture as Findlaech gently pushed the ring onto her finger. It was a perfect fit.

"It was made for you," the jeweller said.

"And I'm never taking it off," Clodagh said turning her hand to look at the ring in more detail.

"I think that's settled then," Findlaech said, taking out his wallet.

Clodagh took his arm and said 'thank you' so many times that Findlaech lost count. He was just about to put his pin number into the little card machine when he heard a slight whimper and Clodagh's arm slipped from his.

She had dropped to the floor like a stone and was now writhing from side to side, her eyes rolling in her head.

Findlaech had never seen Clodagh have one of her seizures, and had been hoping he would never have to, but her father had shown him exactly what to do should it happen. It was important to note exactly how long the seizure lasted so he immediately looked at his watch and took a mental note of the time. He made sure there was nothing close to her that she could hurt herself on and then turned her gently on to her side to keep her airways clear, placing his jacket underneath her head.

"Can you call an ambulance please?" he asked the jeweller, who immediately responded and got on the phone.

Although the seizure only lasted a couple of minutes, Findlaech was concerned because Clodagh had not recovered consciousness and he was very relieved when the paramedics arrived and took over. He explained exactly what had happened and was thankful when they said he should ride in the back of the ambulance in case she came round. It was important that she saw a friendly face.

While they were racing through town with the siren on and blue lights flashing, Findlaech phoned Meabh and told her exactly what had happened. He asked if she could please phone the Quinns and he would keep them posted as to what was happening. His heart was racing, and felt he was probably to blame because he had allowed her to get too excited. He hated seeing her lying there on the stretcher, her face so pale, covered by an oxygen mask. He held her hand and whispered to her that everything would be all right. He was trying to convince himself, he couldn't bear it if anything happened to his princess.

When they drew up outside A&E, the back doors flew open and the paramedics shouted information to the doctor and two nurses who came to take over so they knew exactly what had happened. Findlaech jumped out and followed them into the clinical atmosphere of the hospital building.

Clodagh was immediately placed into a side cubicle, the curtains were drawn across, and Findlaech was asked to go and wait in the waiting room.

"Can't I stay with her?" he pleaded. "She will be so frightened when she comes round. Oh, and you need to call Doctor Fairleigh, he is her consultant."

"Thank you, sir, we will do that now. We will call you as soon as we have made our assessment, in the meantime would you please mind waiting over there. I promise you we are doing everything for your wife."

'Wife', they had called her his wife and the tears rolled down his face as he made his way into the waiting area.

He seemed to have been sitting there for hours when he felt a friendly arm round his shoulders. Meabh had sat down next to him and he hadn't even realised.

"Oh, Meabh, please tell me everything will be all right. I don't want to go on if Clodagh isn't going to be with me," and he buried his head into her chest and allowed the tears to fall.

"Let's not jump to unnecessary conclusions, son, until we have spoken to the doctors. You know she has always recovered from her seizures before."

"Yes, but this time she didn't come round from it and she was such a funny colour," he said in between sobs.

Riley had gone to pick up the Quinns and soon all five of them were sitting in the waiting area, worry lines etched on their faces. After Findlaech had explained exactly what had happened, they all sat in silence, fidgeting, unable to sit still. It was so hard to take on board, Clodagh had been doing so well.

Eventually Doctor Fairleigh came in to see them. He pulled one of the chairs round in front of them and sat with his hands calmly in his lap.

"After I saw Clodagh last time with Findlaech, she was doing so well I suggested that we reduce the medication. I fear now that was the wrong decision. She has suffered what we refer to as a grand mal seizure which has caused an irregular heart rhythm, problems with her breathing and also irregular brain activity. I doubt very much she will remember what has happened and there is a risk of temporary amnesia when she eventually comes round. We won't really know what other side effects there are until she wakes up. In the meantime we are keeping her comfortable and helping her with her breathing."

"She will come round won't she, doctor?" Findlaech asked.

"As long as she has the fight left in her, she will come round, but that will dependent on all your support. Talk to her, even though you might not think she can hear. We have learned from past experience that patients can often hear what is being said to them even though they are not visibly conscious."

"Can we go in and see her?" Mrs Quinn asked, her eyes red from crying.

"We are just moving her up to the ward and once she is settled we will let you visit her, but only two at a time, we don't want to cause too much excitement."

They thanked the doctor and Riley went off to the cafeteria to get everyone a nice cup of tea. When he returned they had all made the decision that her parents would see Clodagh first, then Meabh and Riley and finally, Findlaech, who had told them all he wasn't leaving the hospital until he knew she was all right. He didn't want her waking up on her own.

"Oh and Da, my car is in Quayside Shopping Centre. Is there any way you can get it home for me so I don't end up with a huge fine or it gets towed away?"

"Don't you worry about that, son, we will take care of everything. You concentrate on getting your princess well."

Findlaech stood up and gave Riley a great big hug.

"We are all here for you, son. But you know that don't you."

After everyone had left, Riley went up to the ward where he discovered that they had put Clodagh in a side room on her own. As soon as he opened the door he was taken aback by the number of tubes coming out of her body. There were two up her nose to help her breathe, but there were also several coming out of her arm feeding her intravenous fluids which dripped slowly from the plastic pouches.

"Oh, Clodagh, what have they done to you?"

Findlaech felt like ripping all the tubes out of her and lifting her out of the bed and taking her home. He could take care of her; he could nurse her back to health. Tears rolled down his face and he stood for several seconds before he realised a nurse had come into the room.

"I know, it's a bit of a shock when you see them all wired up, isn't it?" she said kindly.

"Will she be OK, nurse? Please say she will get better."

"Sit down, Findlaech, isn't it?"

Findlaech just nodded and accepted the chair which the nurse had placed beside the bed.

"Talk to her, Findlaech; talk about all the plans you have. Your mother told me you have just got engaged. Congratulations."

Findlaech looked down at her hands and was horrified to see that the ring was missing.

The nurse didn't miss a trick.

"Don't worry, it is safe. Unfortunately we can't leave any jewellery on in case she has to go into theatre for any reason."

The nurse handed Findlaech a little plastic bag that contained the ring and also the little necklace which bore a gold heart containing his picture. He took the little bag and held it to his chest.

"With your love and your strength, Clodagh will get well. I can't promise she will be as strong as before, but you can both get through this."

Findlaech was finding it hard to hold it together, but he knew that tears were not going to help his princess now. He needed to be strong. The nurse was right, together they would get through this.

After the nurse left, Findlaech pulled the chair closer to the bed and spoke softly. He told her that his love was bigger than the entire universe and that she was the half of him that had been missing for so long. He talked and he talked and he talked. He talked about their future, about the holidays they would have together, about the animals on their farm and just how happy they would be.

He didn't know when he had fallen asleep, but he was woken abruptly by a loud beeping noise. He was about to run out of the room and fetch someone when the door burst open and three nurses ran in with a crash cart.

Still not fully awake he just stared at the scene in front of him. He really didn't feel a part of this, it was like the worst nightmare and he was just an onlooker. The nurse who had been so kind to him earlier, took him gently by the arm and led him out of the room.

He didn't remember being helped into a chair, he didn't hear any of the kind words of reassurance being said to him, and he didn't remember spilling the cup of tea down his jeans. Findlaech was in shock and the only way his body knew how to cope with it was to completely shut down. He was numb from head to toe and his brain would not register anything. His world had become black.

20 Where Is The Sun?

The first thing Findlaech remembered was a warm lick on his face. Conan had been lying patiently by his master's side for two days, trying every trick he knew to bring him out of his dark place. He had been like this before, but instead of the horrors of his 'depressions', Findlaech couldn't remember a thing. He remembered doctors rushing into Clodagh's room at the hospital and the dreadful beeping of the machine monitoring her heart, but after that his life was a blank.

He sat bolt upright, his head spinning from the exertion, stress and lack of food for the last few days. As soon as he felt his legs were strong enough to hold him, he got out of bed and went downstairs and into the kitchen. Meabh and Riley were sitting at the breakfast table, steaming cups of tea in front of them.

"She's alright!" he exclaimed.

"What do you mean, son?" Riley asked.

"Clodagh, she's alright. I wouldn't have woken up if she hadn't sent me a message and I have to go."

They both looked at him with a bemused expression.

"Woa, slow down. Sit down and explain exactly what you mean," Meabh said pulling a chair out and guiding him to sit down. She immediately poured him a hot, sweet cup of tea and placed it in front of him.

Findlaech was frustrated that they didn't understand. Had he been in a better frame of mind he would have realised that to anyone else it sounded like jibberish, but he knew their bond was so strong, Clodagh had talked to him.

"Right, before you start talking, you need to get some food down you. You will be too weak to go anywhere and don't start arguing because I will physically hold you down until you do," Meabh said with more force than she intended.

It had been an awful three days and she had found it hard to eat herself, but she knew they had to stay strong for Findlaech. Clodagh had hung onto life after they restarted her heart, but the reports back from her parents were that it was touch and go and that she may never recover use of the left hand side of her body. Even worse was the doctor's warning that her brain could be severely damaged following the seizure and the resulting stroke. Of course Findlaech knew nothing of this and now was not the time to tell him. He had a fire in his eyes which had been missing since they bought him back from the hospital, and neither of them intended to dampen his optimism.

Surprisingly, Findlaech tucked into a full breakfast of bacon, sausage, egg, mushrooms, tomato and fried bread, washed down by three cups of tea. When he had finished he wiped his mouth and looked at his ma and pa.

"If you don't mind I really don't want to have to explain now. I am going to have a bath and a shave and smarten myself up and then I am off to the hospital."

"I shall drive you, son, I am not sure you are strong enough to take yourself," Riley said.

"Thank you, Da, that would be great," and he vanished upstairs.

"What do you make of what he said?" Meabh asked.

"I am not sure, Meabh, I am not really sure . . ."

Riley dropped Findlaech at the hospital and told him to call when he was ready to be picked up. Findlaech didn't want to wait for the lift to take him to the third floor, instead he took the stairs. He knew for certain that Clodagh was going to be alright, otherwise why would she have come to him in his dream and spoken to him. He had never experienced anything like it before and now he was positive everything was going to be OK.

When he reached her room, the same nurse who had comforted him earlier that week was checking Clodagh's chart. Clodagh was still the same with all the tubes helping her stay alive, but at least there was a tinge of pink on her cheeks which was missing before.

"Hello, Findlaech, you look a lot better than when I last saw you," she said with a friendly smile on her face.

"I feel so much better now, thank you. It was all too much of a shock seeing my girl like that. Everything will be all right now."

"What makes you say that, Findlaech?" she asked.

"Because she spoke to me and told me not to worry," he said, suddenly realising how silly that sounded. "And I am not going mad before you ask. She spoke to me in my dream and I know she is fighting to stay alive. She has too much to live for to give up the fight."

"I don't think you are mad, Findlaech. In fact it is that sort of positive attitude that will pull a coma patient back to the present. I am going to leave you now because I know you will have a lot to say to her."

"Thank you, Ruby," Findlaech said, reading the name tag on her uniform, "you have been so kind to us. She couldn't have done this without your special care and attention." Totally out of character, Findlaech leaned forward and gave her a gentle kiss on the cheek. "I owe you so much."

Ruby was flattered and said that she could see Clodagh was a very special person.

Findlaech drew the chair over to the side of the bed and took Clodagh's limp hand in his. He stroked it and started to talk to her about his dream and how he had heard her voice.

"I know you are trying to tell me something and I am listening. You can't give up now because you love me too much, I know that. Conan knows as well because he woke me up this morning and encouraged me to get out of bed. You know he is one wise mutt. I have your ring safe in my pocket and as soon as you wake up it is going back on your finger where it belongs. And I know we said we would wait a couple of years before we got married, but I can't wait and I am going to make sure it happens this summer come what may."

He stopped talking suddenly as he felt a slight squeeze of his hand.

"Clodagh, do that again."

He hadn't imagined it, there it was, she had moved her hand.

He was about to call out to the nurse, when he noticed her eyes starting to flutter. Little by little they opened and she blinked several times as she tried to focus on her surroundings.

"Clodagh, Clodagh, I knew you could do it. Take it slowly I am here with you."

She made a small whimpering noise as if she was trying to speak, but Findlaech said "Shhh" and gave her a gentle kiss on her forehead. "Don't try and talk, let me tell you what happened."

He explained everything that had happened to her in the last few days, but told her it was going to be all right. He must have been talking for about twenty minutes when the nurse returned with Clodagh's doctor for his daily rounds.

"Ah, I see our patient is awake," he said kindly.

"I think she would like to talk, but it is hard with that tube down her throat, is it possible to take it out?" Findlaech asked.

In truth, the doctor was surprised to see such recognition in his patient's eyes, he had expected so much worse.

"Can we have half an hour with Clodagh please, then we will call you back in?" the doctor said.

"As long as you promise to take out that nasty tube," he replied smiling.

Once again Findlaech went to wait in the seating area, but this time he did not feel desolate and alone, his world was not painted black, there were bright colours, cheerful sounds and most of all he had his Clodagh back.

By the time he was allowed to return to her room, the change in her was remarkable. She had been propped up into a sitting position with plenty of pillows supporting her back and head. As he walked into the room her face lit up in a smile.

"I told you I'd be back," he said returning her smile.

Her voice was croaky and he had to lean close to her to hear exactly what she was saying, but he distinctly heard, "You heard me then. I was trying to get through to you for days but you wouldn't let me in."

"Yes, I heard you. I was in a very dark place but you were the one who bought me back."

The doctor and nurse were both astounded at what they heard. He knew they this pair had somehow worked miracles on one another, but this was beyond belief. They suddenly realised the strength of the bond between them.

Findlaech turned to the nurse and said, "Miracles *do* happen."

"We are going to leave you alone now, but I will be back later to discuss Clodagh's rehabilitation and I would like you to be here, Findlaech, if that's all right."

"I won't be going anywhere doctor, at least not without my princess."

As soon as they were alone, Findlaech reached into his pocket and took out the sparkling diamond ring and placed it gently on her left hand. Clodagh's face was a picture and then he saw a tear run down her cheek.

"Why are you sad, my love?" he said, worried that she had changed her mind.

"Because I can't move my left arm. How am I going to show off my ring to everyone?"

"You silly billy, that is only temporary. We are going to work and work until we can work no more until you can use that left arm. Nothing can stop us now, Clodagh."

"You are right, Findlaech, nothing can stop us now."

The sun streamed through the window lighting their world.

Clodagh had to stay for another eight weeks in the hospital while she received physio to help her walk again and regain partial use in her left arm. She also worked with a therapist to improve her speech which had become a little slurred but was improving with each day. Findlaech was with her every step of the way, encouraging and pushing her when she started to get tired. They had talked about getting married in August and that was their goal, to get her well enough to walk down the aisle of The Church of The Most Holy Rosary where they had both been baptised.

Day by day Clodagh started to regain her strength. They started making plans and couldn't wait for the day she was allowed home. The future was looking bright again.

21 The Butterfly

The whole of Aclare talked about the miracle that had happened at Sligo General Hospital. When Clodagh arrived home she received so many cards and flowers they didn't know where to put them. Clodagh had always been the little wilting wallflower and had no idea just how caring people could be. Findlaech had made her see life in a different light and, so long as he was with her, she knew she would be fine. She could now talk quite freely without having to think about each word before she formed it, but she still needed a stick to help her walk.

It was less than a month to their wedding and she was getting frustrated with her progress. Everyone was so encouraging and saying that she was doing so well, but for Clodagh it was not enough. She needed to be fit and well to become Findlaech's wife; at the moment she felt more of a burden. Doubts started to creep into her troubled mind and she started to withdraw into her shell, like a hermit crab escaping the incoming waves.

Everyone noticed the change in her; most of all Findlaech. Despite all his words of encouragement he couldn't seem to bring back his bright, loving, laughing princess. He was at a loss as to what to do. He needed to come up with a brainwave to help her out of this situation and he would never give up even if it took him forever.

Back at home he talked with his ma and pa to see if they had any ideas on what he could do.

"Ma, she keeps saying she will be nothing but a burden to

me and it doesn't matter how many times I tell her what she means to me and that she would never be a burden, I can't seem to get through to her."

"You will think of something, son, no one knows Clodagh better than you," Meabh said.

Findlaech had a restless night, he just couldn't think of anything that would prove just how important Clodagh was to him. He tossed and turned and in the end gave up trying to sleep and decided to take Conan out for walk to try and clear his head. He put on his outdoor clothes, picked up a torch and nearly fell over Conan as he rushed to get to the back door first.

They walked across the meadow, past the bog where Conan had got stuck, past the ridge on the mountain where Snowy had been stranded and on to one of the higher ridges that gave them a view of the sea – or would have done if it had been light enough.

When they reached the top, Findlaech sat down on the soft, mossy grass and looked out towards the ocean, his arm around Conan who leaned against him. As they waited the sky started to change colour as the sun started to poke its nose out of the horizon.

"I know what to do, Conan. I will need your help, though."

They walked back home and were welcomed by the smell of breakfast as they opened the back door.

Meabh and Riley both looked up, but neither said anything. They knew instinctively he was fighting mentally to try and come up with a solution.

Meabh just placed a steaming cup of tea in his normal

place, followed by a plate of bubble and squeak with a fried egg on top and two nicely browned sausages.

Findlaech said nothing until he had finished eating. "I know exactly what I have to do. Thank you for breakfast, Ma, but if you don't mind I have to go out to the barn, I have something to make."

"Need any help, son," Riley said smiling.

"When you are ready. Two pairs of hands are always better than one."

By the time Riley got out to the barn Findlaech had assembled many pieces of wood and had taken down the old wooden sled from the rafters, the one he had used so often as a child with his brother.

"Da, I am going to convert this old sled into a magnificent carriage so that Conan and I can pull Clodagh up into the hills."

Riley just nodded and they set to work.

When they told Meabh what they were doing, she made some plump cushions and filled them with duck down, and a lovely fur throw out of an old fur coat that had been handed down through her family. She didn't condone the killing of animals to make clothing, but she was certain a throw to keep Clodagh warm would be acceptable.

They worked tirelessly for two days until Findlaech was satisfied the carriage was fit for his princess.

The forecast for the afternoon was dry and sunny, and as the weather could change in an instant over the mountains of Aclare, Findlaech knew he couldn't wait.

He drove his little Mini over the bumpy old track as fast

as he dared until he arrived outside Clodagh's house. He ran up to the front door and rapped loudly. Mrs Quinn answered the door and gave Findlaech the biggest hug. "Oh, Findlaech, I am so glad you are hear she is having such a bad day. I think because you haven't been to see her in a couple of days she won't even come out of her room."

"I am sorry Mrs Quinn, I probably should have explained what I was doing. I will never, I repeat NEVER, abandon your daughter and I hope after today I can change her mind about feeling useless."

"Oh, Findlaech, if anyone can do it you can."

Findlaech ran up the stairs two at a time and knocked gently on Clodagh's bedroom door. There was no answer. He knocked again and waited. Again there was no answer. He could hear the sound of muffled sobs coming from inside and he didn't wait any longer. He opened the door and before she had time to say anything, he picked her up gently in his arms and carried her down to the car.

Mrs Quinn was one step ahead and opened the car door so that Findlaech could put Clodagh on the front seat. Her eyes were red from crying and she was ringing a sodden handkerchief in her hands. She looked up at her mother as Findlaech was about to close the door. "Have faith Clodagh," her mother said and gave her the warmest smile.

Clodagh wasn't ready for talking and Findlaech knew this. He had often been in a very dark place and the last thing he wanted to do was talk. So they drove in silence until he pulled up in the yard and gave a little toot on the horn.

As he did, Conan and Goliath, led by Riley, pulled out

the carriage which was indeed now fit for a princess. Both the animals were behaving impeccably, aware that this was a momentous occasion.

As promised the sun was shining and there wasn't a single rain cloud in the sky. It wasn't that warm for July, but Findlaech was unconcerned because his Ma had made sure Clodagh would be warm and comfortable.

He gently lifted her out of the car and carried her over to the carriage. He pulled back the fur throw, and made sure she was comfortable with a big cushion under her bottom to lessen the bumps and a big one behind her back and to support her head. Meabh had made a picnic hamper which she placed on the shelf they had specially prepared at the back of the old sled. Clodagh was wide eyed and silent, but at least she had stopped crying.

Findlaech stepped into the old horse harness, and attached it to the front of the sled so that he was the lead in the threesome. It wasn't exactly a golden carriage with three white horses, but it was better than that, it was one made specially for his own princess.

Meabh and Riley both gave Clodagh a kiss on the cheek and waved them off. On the flat ground the carriage moved easily, with Findlaech taking care not to hit too many rocks. They went past the bog where Conan had been stuck and also past the rocky ledge where Snowy had been precariously balanced, and Findlaech talked about all the adventures he'd had with his animals as they went. He told her how he had made a harness out of old string and gaffer tape, and another rope to pull Conan out of the bog. He told her how he had been so frightened that Meabh and Riley would desert him, but instead they had adopted him. He told her about his new sister and her baby and about how wonderful it was when they were all together at Christmas. But most of all he told her the very best day in his life was the day he had met Clodagh at the market. He talked and talked, until his voice was hoarse and he was starting to puff as they ascended the final hill.

It was a hard struggle as his feet tried to find purchase on the uneven ground. Conan and Goliath remained stoic throughout, aware their master was reliant on their efforts. Together they pulled and pulled until eventually they arrived at the top. Totally out of breath, Findlaech released the two animals so that Goliath could go and eat some sweet fresh grass and Conan could get a drink out of the fresh water cascading down the side of the hill.

When he was happy they were settled, he removed the fur cover from Clodagh's legs and laid it on the grass. Then, as if she were made of glass, he lifted her out and laid her on the rug, putting the big cushions behind her so that she could sit up comfortably.

The hamper had got a little shaken up, but thankfully the contents weren't too badly damaged. He poured two glasses of Meabh's fresh lemonade and laid the sandwiches, cakes and other goodies out on a clean tea towel.

Clodagh in all this time had still not uttered a word, but Findlaech could see she was a lot more relaxed and she had some colour in her cheeks. He didn't ask her anything, he respected her silence. He just talked about his adventures before he had met her. He leaned to one side and picked a perfect specimen of a bright yellow cowslip. He held Clodagh's hand, opened her fingers and laid the flower in the palm of her hand.

"This little wild flower, in all its perfection, is how I see you Clodagh. I see you as a butterfly. Beautiful, perfect and unblemished. No matter what happens in life, we can get through this together. I am tarnished, I am not perfect, but you accepted me for who I am. I will have my black days. I will have days when I probably won't talk to you, but it doesn't mean I stop loving you. You are as precious to me as all the nature that surrounds us now. The flowers surviving against all odds in this windy place, the sea that never stops its ebb and flow, the sun that tries to find a place in the sky and the rain that gives life to everything. That is what you mean to me. Can't you see that?"

At that very moment Conan came and sat next to Clodagh and leaned his body against hers. He placed a paw on her leg and licked her hand gently. Then the second miracle happened, a beautiful, rare, Marsh fritillary butterfly landed on the top of Clodagh's head.

"Will you just look at that, Clodagh, I said you were my beautiful butterfly."

Findlaech didn't dare look at Clodagh, he had no idea whether his words had penetrated or not. He felt her body shaking next to his and he became frightened; so frightened that he had said too much and that he had made her cry.

He felt a hand softly touch his cheek and then he turned his head. To his complete surprise, Clodagh was not crying, she was shaking because she was laughing.

He leant forward and kissed her so gently on the lips. She responded and pulled him towards her.

"I have been so silly, Findlaech, I now see that your love is bigger than any of the mountains in Aclare."

Findlaech's heart skipped a beat.

22 Stalemate

Father Boyle was adamant, "NO animals!" and it didn't matter how Findlaech pleaded he wouldn't budge. He was a good priest and had listened over the years to his parishioners' problems, but to fill his church with animals went against all his beliefs.

Clodagh was insistent that Conan was at their wedding because she had been training him to hold one side of her train, while little Cara would take the other.

"Not even one dog?" Findlaech asked again.

"Not even one dog, Findlaech. This is a wedding that is sacred and it shouldn't involve animals."

"But they are not just animals, Father, these are our children, our friends and most of all Clodagh wants Conan to be there."

They seemed to be at stalemate. Father Boyle would not change his views and Findlaech was not prepared to let Clodagh down.

"In that case, Father, I am afraid we will have to find somewhere else to get married."

"But the Quinns have always come to this church. I don't think they will be happy if there daughter gets married elsewhere."

"The Quinns will be happy if their daughter is happy, so unless you are prepared to bend the rules a little, I will be making other arrangements."

Findlaech didn't usually get cross, but today he felt a little frustrated at the priest's stilted and rather old-fashioned attitude. He didn't want to argue with him so he just turned and walked away before he said something he regretted. He would talk this over with his Ma and Pa, the Quinns, but most of all Clodagh.

Meabh decided to invite them all over for afternoon tea to discuss the matter. She was in total agreement with Findlaech and Clodagh that Conan should be allowed to attend, after all he wasn't just some wayward dog, he had saved his master's life on more than one occasion.

They all sat round the kitchen table because that had always been where important decisions were made. Tea and Irish barm brack were the refreshments, the topic of discussion – what they should do about the wedding venue.

"Maybe you should back down, Clodagh, there is no point in upsetting Father Boyle," Mrs Quinn said addressing her daughter.

"No, Ma, I don't see why I should. Conan always has our backs and I know for certain that his feelings would be hurt if he wasn't included in the ceremony."

"I am inclined to agree with Clodagh. Having lived with Conan I know just how special he is," Meabh said.

"Then in that case we will need to find a venue where we can get married and animals *are* allowed," Findlaech said.

"I have been looking into this," Riley came into the conversation. "If we register our marriage legally at the registry office in Sligo, then we could have an informal wedding ceremony here at the feirme conducted by a celebrant. We don't have time to apply for a marriage venue licence, so I think that would probably be the answer."

"Yes... yes... yes... That would be the answer. I would so love to get married here and I know it would be extra special for Findlaech because he has struggled with his faith over the past few years," Clodagh said taking his hand. "Do we have time to organise it all?"

"Leave it with us," Meabh said. "You are going to have a wedding to remember. No, I correct myself, a wedding that no one will ever forget."

The Quinns weren't totally convinced, but seeing their daughter so happy, how could they object. However, Mr Quinn insisted that he needed to be involved in all the preparations and so they all shook hands in total agreement.

The next few weeks were a hustle and bustle of activity on everyone's part. Clodagh had already chosen her dress and Meabh was altering it slightly as it had been a bit too long and rather too loose around the waist.

Riley and Findlaech were working on making an altar out of pieces of oak, while Meabh was making swathes of white silk to hang over it. They also made a platform out of wood which they painted white and Meabh had made beautiful silk flowers to compliment the lilies which they had ordered from a flower shop in Sligo. Mr Quinn, who on his own admission was not very good with his hands, made sure all the necessary paperwork was in order.

They made six large trestle tables which Meabh was going to laden with goodies. Both men had objected, saying that it was much too much for one person to do, but Meabh had been adamant they wouldn't be eating anyone else's food on that day, it had to be perfect. They knew better than to argue with her.

Riley was being a bit secretive about certain things, but Findlaech knew better than to badger him. He knew he always did things for a reason, so why should he question his decisions.

Finally, they could all take a break as everything was ready and they could put their feet up. The wedding was to take place in two days' time when the weather forecast was perfect. Clodagh had not been allowed to come to the feirme because they didn't want her to see what they had done. Although she was a bit disappointed, she knew it would be extra special if she waited until her wedding day.

23 My heart can't take it

It was a Thursday and the weather was perfect, not even a breeze to blow the tablecloths off the trestle tables. Mrs Quinn was busy arranging flowers as centrepieces on all the tables, while Meabh put the finishing touches to the wedding cake. Riley was doing something secretive in the barn and told Meabh that Findlaech wasn't to come in on any account, while keeping one eye on little Cara while she played with a wooden horse he had made for her. Niamh was with Clodagh helping her get ready.

Findlaech had been told to stay out of the way so he decided the best thing he could do was go for a walk with Conan to try and calm his nerves. He kept worrying that she would change her mind and not turn up for some reason, and it was making him very edgy.

Walking across the fields full of wild flowers and watching nature go about its daily business helped to take his mind off the wedding. He always felt calm when he was close to nature. Conan was more than happy to be out with his master, pouncing on grasshoppers as they chirruped in the long grass and trying his damnedest to catch a butterfly.

Findlaech sat down on a clump of glass, ran his hands through his thick hair and sighed. He had woken with only positive thoughts in his head but somehow he could not shake off this feeling of impending doom. He knew Clodagh loved him with all her heart, but so much of her confidence had been taken away from her since she had her stroke. She had made so much progress in the last few weeks and her speech was nearly back to normal, but he knew inside her head she wasn't perfect enough to walk down the aisle as his bride. All he could do was show her how much he loved her and that nothing was going to stop them from being together. He truly hoped he had convinced her.

Findlaech had never worn a watch, but he could always tell you the time within a few minutes. Today the sun hadn't reached its height in the sky and the ceremony was taking place at midday.

"Right, Conan, enough of these negative thoughts. You are always positive, my friend, and I shall follow your example. Let's go and get ready."

He barked in acknowledgement and started running back towards home.

Everyone was so busy with their allotted duties they hadn't noticed the pair arrive back at the feirme. He went upstairs with Conan at his heels and ran a deep bath, even spoiling himself with some of his Ma's bath salts. He sank into the steamy water, lay his head back against the end of the bath and closed his eyes. He allowed his breaths to get deeper and deeper until he had calmed his mind.

Suddenly something landed on top of him causing the water to overflow onto the floor.

"Conan, you idiot, what on earth are you doing?"

Conan knew his master was unsettled. He needed to get close to him and the only way he knew how was to actually lay on top of his body; that way he could help calm his breathing.

"You fool, Conan, I am not having one of my bad days, just a few niggling doubts," but Conan was having none of it and he edged his way up his master's body until he could lick his face.

"Oh well, while you are in here you might as well have a bath as well," and he laughed.

Conan, believing he had helped his master out of the doldrums, was quite happy to have his body massaged. The bathroom was in a terrible state by the time they had finished. There was water everywhere and each time Conan shook, droplets shot up the walls, over the mirror and turned the tiled floor into a skating rink.

Meabh, hearing a commotion upstairs, knocked on the door and waited for Findlaech to answer. When she saw the state of the bathroom instead of being cross she laughed out loud. "You two will be the death of me. Now be gone while I clear up this mess. Go and get ready."

"Oh Ma, you are simply the best," and he kissed her very hard on the cheek. "You'll have my wife to fuss over soon."

They had decided it would be safer if Clodagh came to live with them so that when Findlaech was out working, Meabh would still be around to keep an eye on her until she got her strength back. Of course she was delighted, she wouldn't be losing her son, in fact she was gaining another daughter.

Findlaech was starting to pace. It was already twelve fifteen and there had been no sign of Clodagh. His Da had left an hour ago to go and pick her up and he was starting to fear something dreadful had happened. He was close to tears and didn't know what to do. Everyone was seated facing the homemade altar, the celebrant was waiting at the side and the string quartet Niamh had hired were playing softly trying to keep everyone calm.

Conan had picked up on his master's agitation and was starting to run round in circles. Findlaech was about to reprimand him when Meabh came over and said, "Why don't you let him go and find out what has happened."

"Really ... a dog?" said the celebrant.

"This is no ordinary dog, Mr Brynn, this is Conan," Meabh said indignantly. "Go, Conan, go find Clodagh."

He didn't need telling twice and ran out of the yard, up the lane as fast as his four legs would carry him. The bow around his neck was really annoying, but he knew his master wanted him to look that way so he tried to ignore it.

He got to the end of the lane and looked both ways. No sign of Clodagh or Riley so he headed down the road towards her house. He had been running for about ten minutes when he stopped dead. Standing in front of him was a beautiful white horse, with a long flowing mane. The horse was attached to a sleigh which was covered in white faux fur and Clodagh was sitting on top looking as pretty as a picture, albeit at a slant.

One of the wheels that Riley had replaced the runners with had hit a bolder on the side of the road and had buckled badly. Mr Quinn and Riley were bending over seeing if there was any way they could fix it, but they knew it was hopeless.

"I will run home and get my car," Mr Quinn said. "Don't worry sweetheart we will get you there by hook or by crook."

"Da, I don't want to arrive by car. This is the only time I will get married and I want to arrive in style."

At first Riley thought she was being a bit petulant until she told them exactly what she wanted to do. "I want to ride the horse to my wedding," she said to their surprise.

"Ride the horse?" both men said in unison.

"Do you honestly think that is wise?" Mr Quinn said, leaving off the bit he was thinking about 'in her state of health'.

"Riley, please unhook the horse from my carriage and help my Da lift me up."

They both stood dumbfounded.

"Riley, please help me, I know you understand."

He nodded and started to unhitch the horse from the sleigh.

Conan, in the meantime, had grabbed the horse's reins and was holding on tight, determined that Snowflake wasn't going anywhere until they were ready.

Mr Quinn lifted his daughter down from the sleigh and then with Riley's help they managed to lift her up until she was sitting astride the mare.

With Riley supporting her on one side, Mr Quinn supporting her on the other and Conan leading the horse they made their way down the road and turned into the lane leading to the feirme. Snowflake placed each hoof carefully, trying not to slip on the loose stones or twist a fetlock down one of the many potholes; she was well aware she was carrying a very special load.

Findlaech could not believe his eyes when he saw the horse turn into the yard. It was a vision to turn anyone's heart and he felt the tears of pride and joy well up in his eyes. Instead of being lifted down Clodagh asked if she could ride the horse up to the altar with Conan leading her. The two men stepped away and allowed the threesome to make their way down the aisle as everyone looked on in amazement. Everyone held their breath until they finally reached the altar and then they all let out a sigh of a relief.

Findlaech lifted Clodagh down as if she were made of glass and then stood next to her at the altar, surrounded by all the beautiful flowers.

"That was quite some entrance," he whispered into her ear.

"It was perfect," she replied and took his hand.

The celebrant was about to begin the ceremony when a very red-faced Father Boyle came scurrying into the yard. He ran down between all the guests until he reached the altar.

"I am sorry Mr Brynn, but I could never forgive myself if I didn't marry these two very special people. Would you allow me to take over?"

Mr Brynn was about to hand over the sheet with his wording, when Father Boyle turned to him and said, "I won't be needing your words, thank you, I have it all up here in my head."

It was the start of what turned out to be the most perfect day.

Printed in Great Britain
by Amazon

52423860R00116